WINTER'S CAPTIVE

THE LOCHLANN TREATY
BOOK ONE

ROBIN D. MAHLE
ELLE MADISON

Cover by Covers by Combs

Copy Editing by Holmes Edits

Proofreading by Kate Anderson

Map by Elle Madison

"You walked into the room and now my heart has been stolen

You took me back in time to when I was unbroken

Now you're all I want

And I knew it from the very first moment

Cause a light came on when I heard that song and I want you to sing it again"

— JAMES ARTHUR

THE WEDDING

I stared down at my dirt-covered hands. Blood trickled from a cut on my palm onto my beautiful wedding gown, the red contrasting starkly against pristine white velvet.

I hadn't even registered falling. All I felt was the frigid chill that sank deep into my bones.

Still, I couldn't seem to bring myself to move from this spot. It was supposed to be my wedding day. It was supposed to be the happiest day of my life.

But something had gone very wrong. My fiancé was gone, maybe even dead, and I had no idea how to get to him.

I had been moments away from walking down the aisle when they brought me the news. The Prince of Luan was gone.

Taken.

I ran toward his bedchamber, ignoring the shouts behind me.

No...

I stumbled through the castle, losing a shoe on the grand staircase and somehow tearing my dress somewhere along the way.

Not my Oliver...

Bursting through his door, I stopped short at the sight of his room in shambles. His trunk had been sacked and flipped over, the wood splintered, the lock broken. His clothes were everywhere. The bedcovers were torn and thrown about the room. A lamp lay broken on the floor, oil pooling around shards of glass.

My chest tightened. *He fought, struggled to stay with me. How did no one hear? How did no one see?*

Something swayed in the corner of my vision, catching my eye. A flag had been left on the mantle, an imposing black X against a red backdrop. The symbol of the Aramach.

My breath hitched. *The rebels have him.*

Everything after that was a blur. I remember mumbling something about needing some air, and the next thing I knew, I was outside.

I had staggered to the sprawling willow tree — my tree — and fallen beside its naked, cascading branches. I stayed there, stunned, unable to go any farther.

And now I was freezing. *How long have I been out here?* The biting cold had reddened my hands and numbed my skin, while violent shivers wracked my body.

Tears fell unbidden. I looked up at the sky, as if that would stop their flow, and a single snowflake fell onto my eyelashes in response. How could something so tiny, so delicate, seem to hold such weight?

A soft, bittersweet laugh escaped my lips. I had wanted it to snow today. I loved the snow. But this small flake felt like a betrayal.

I was supposed to be married today. It was supposed to be the happiest day of my life.

Instead, my world had been shattered.

CHAPTER 1

The Morning Before

"The Aramach have been causing trouble for the outer villages near Bala Dam again, Sire." Captain Brodie's demeanor was calm when he spoke to my father, but the barest undercurrent of exasperation laced his tone and a minuscule twitch disturbed his graying whiskers.

He must have been concerned enough to interrupt our weekly petitions with this news, but it hardly seemed urgent. The curious faces of our people, everyone from nobles to villagers, peered at the exchange from the edges of the throne room.

My family and I held open court once a week. It was my favorite day, both because of the opportunity to do something good for my people and the rare chance to spend time with both of my parents.

"They are nothing but an inept ragtag group of children who aspire to be revolutionaries." My father frowned. "Send a group to root them out and put an end to their antics. This is the last I expect to hear of it, Captain." He looked every inch the King of H'Ria. His dark waves were arranged perfectly under a golden crown set with emeralds. While his posture appeared relaxed and unbothered by the news he'd received, his regal amber eyes were narrowed in annoyance.

I was surprised he wasn't taking our respected captain more seriously, but it was hardly my place to say so. Even though I would be crowned Queen in just over a month's time, the daily running of the kingdom would still fall largely to my father.

"Right away, Sire." Captain Brodie didn't falter under my father's gaze. He was the epitome of a warrior, from his battle scars and missing hand to his proud, unruffled posture. After a moment, he bowed and exited the throne room, his expression unchanging.

I understood his frustration. The idea of the Aramach was frightening enough, though they sounded like faerie stories: Rebels who materialized from nowhere, appearing in the outer villages without warning, wreaking havoc, and disappearing just as suddenly.

My father wasn't wrong, however. They should hardly pose a significant threat to the entire might of H'Ria.

Soon to be the might of H'Ria and Luan combined.

My union to Oliver would unite the kingdoms once more, under our rulership. The coronation would take place only five short weeks after our marriage ceremony.

I'm getting married tomorrow.

I could feel my heart beat faster at the thought, and the corner of my mouth quirked up in a small grin.

My fate had been decided the week I was born, along with Oliver's and the future of two feuding kingdoms. The treaty would reunite H'Ria and Luan into the Lochlann realm, ending decades of civil war, all with one union.

Arranged marriages weren't uncommon for either of our kingdoms. That Oliver and I were actually in love, though, was a rarity and not something I took for granted.

The warmth of my mother's hand gently rested on mine. Her slender fingers applied just enough pressure to grab my attention, all while never looking away from the villager speaking to her — us. A subtle reminder to stop my daydreaming.

Sitting up straighter, I allowed myself one final moment to swoon before turning my attention back to the business of the throne room.

Still, even years of lessons in decorum couldn't quash my hopeful grin.

I WAS STILL AWAKE LONG AFTER THE REST OF CASTLE Chridhe had fallen asleep when I heard a tentative knocking. Placing the book I'd been reading on the side table, I got up from my favorite overstuffed chair and rushed over to answer. Footsteps receded before I made it to the door, but a note had been slipped under it.

I grinned wildly at the twice-folded piece of paper. My name was written on top in Oliver's flowing penmanship. He wanted to meet.

Heart racing, I was nearly all the way to the passageway before I realized I was wearing nothing but a sheer nightdress. Still, I was too excited to do more than throw a fur cloak over my shoulders. Pausing only long enough to slip my feet into my similarly fur-lined slippers, I skipped over to my fireplace.

The heavy tapestry there hid a narrow doorway. It had been built years ago as a means of escape from danger, and when I found it as a child, I had indeed escaped through it many times. It was far from the only secret passage in the castle, but as far as I knew, it was a family route, one of very few the guards were unaware of.

I padded as quickly as possible down the narrow stone hall, careful to keep my breathing even and my balance steady. The last thing I needed was to trip and wake up the entire castle. I shook my head. If my parents or brother caught me sneaking to his room they were bound to think this was a far more scandalous visit than it would be.

Custom dictated that brides and grooms should not see each other the night before the wedding. Oliver and his convoy had only arrived late this afternoon, and he had been whisked away to his rooms before we could catch a glimpse of one another. A single day would have been one thing, but half a year had gone by since we'd been together and I could hardly sleep knowing he was under the same roof and I still hadn't seen him. Apparently, he felt the same.

When I reached the hall leading to Oliver's bedchamber, his door was ajar. I beamed, certain he had left it that way for me. As I neared, though, low voices drifted through the small opening.

"... the best for you. Your happiness is important to me."

Oliver's Uncle Earc was just behind the door, facing away from me. He had a hand clasped on Oli's shoulder while they spoke. I didn't know the man very well. Business had kept Earc at his estate during most of my visits to the Luanian castle, but I knew Oliver viewed the former war hero as a second father, and that was enough for me.

Not wanting to intrude on this tender moment, I turned to walk away, but Oliver caught sight of me. His eyebrows raised just as the door whipped open. The older, dark-haired man moved into the hallway and gave me a polite bow.

"Your Highness," he greeted. "Lovely to see you again, sweetheart."

I gave a slight nod of my head, my cheeks flushing at being caught presumably eavesdropping, and in my night-dress no less.

"Thank you, Laird Earc." I mustered up a smidgen of

dignity. "I'm pleased that you made the journey to celebrate with us."

"I would not miss it, Highness." His gaze lingered on my frame a bit longer than I was comfortable with.

"Uncle." Oliver coughed, interrupting the awkwardness.

The older man turned back to my fiancé, clapping him on the back. "Goodnight then, son. We will speak later."

We watched as Earc rounded the corner down the hall, then finally turned to face each other.

"I'm sorry, Oli… I had only just walked to the door. I didn't know your uncle would be here." I stumbled over my words a bit, my cheeks reddening at how my practically sprinting to be here had interrupted his time with his uncle.

I probably should have waited.

Oliver responded by taking several large strides toward me, pulling me into his arms. He nudged his door closed with his foot and held on to me for a long while without speaking. I breathed in deeply, contentedly.

He was tall and lean, with his dark waves swept back, accentuating eyes the color of the midwinter sky. He really was the consummate royal. More than being merely gorgeous, though, Oli always made me laugh.

I savored this moment, inhaling his familiar scent of cinnamon and vanilla. Heat flushed through my body.

Oliver sighed in my ear. One of his hands ran lazy circles down my back while the other played with the loose curls at the end of my braid.

"Tomorrow suddenly feels too far away," I murmured, looking up at him.

A long moment of silence passed between us while Oliver continued to play with my plait, eyes glossed over as if he hadn't heard a word I said.

"Oli?"

"Yes. It certainly does." He laughed, his breath suddenly warm against my cheek. "I'm sorry, love. It's a bit difficult to think clearly when you're in my arms like this. I asked you here because I haven't seen you all day and I just wanted... to say goodnight." He smirked.

"Oh? Well, goodnight then." I laughed a little and turned away teasingly, knowing he wouldn't have sent for me only to have me leave so soon.

"Indeed," he said, grabbing my arm and spinning me back to face him, "but I'm afraid that just won't do. In fact, I'm certain I can think of a better way to end the evening." He pulled my chin up and placed his lips on mine.

Before I could halfheartedly mumble something about needing to go, he startled me by backing my body against the wall next to the giant oak door. Our lips met again, more firmly this time. We had kissed before, but rarely with this sense of urgency and desire passing between every point of physical contact.

Stars, I could get used to this.

His hands trailed from my shoulders to the waistline of my pale, thin nightdress, knocking my cloak to the floor in one swift motion. He pulled me in even closer, but it wasn't enough. Picking me up and walking me to the bed, Oliver sat me down on the warm furs, never taking his mouth off mine.

He gripped the curves of my hips as he moved his mouth from my lips down to the base of my neck.

My eyes shot open with the realization of what we were allowing. I bit my lip and forced myself to speak up before we went too far.

"Oliver," I whispered. It took more strength than I knew I possessed to bring myself to stop this.

He moved to lay me back on the bed, but I brought my hand up, placed it on his chest, and said his name with more conviction.

"Oli. I — I should go. We should both rest before tomorrow." The words came out barely above a whisper.

Though we would be married tomorrow, I knew my father might just risk the treaty if he found me in the prince's room, in the prince's bed, with the prince's mouth on my neck.

I leaned up and placed a gentle kiss on his forehead.

His chest rose and fell rapidly as he looked away from me. "Of course. I'm sorry, Charlotte."

Oliver's use of my full name took me by surprise. Usually I was just Charlie. Remorse washed over me when I realized I had just hurt his feelings.

Brilliant, Charlie.

"Oli—"

"It's fine, love." He cut me off, giving me a cocky grin and a wink. "My apologies. I'm afraid I find you quite irresistible."

"And I you, apparently." I laughed a little and placed my hand on his cheek. "Just one more day."

"One more day." He repeated my words with a tinge of sadness.

I smiled softly, grateful that starting tomorrow we would never have to leave each other again.

"I love you," I whispered, reluctantly turning to go.

Our wedding truly couldn't come soon enough.

CHAPTER 2

I awoke to my mother sitting next to me on the bed. Melancholy in her emerald eyes quickly gave way to warmth when she saw me watching her. I quirked an eyebrow, and she shook her head, a small, rueful smile on her face.

"It's simply hard to believe the babe I held in my arms so many years ago is getting married today."

I shot up in my bed. *I'm getting married today.*

A cursory knock sounded at the door, but whoever it was didn't bother to wait for a response. My best friend's fiery curls were the first thing I caught sight of before her tiny body came into view. Several servants followed in her buoyant wake.

From their disgruntled expressions, and the way many of them were still smoothing out aprons or readjusting their frocks, it appeared she had barreled over them in her quest to reach my chambers. Not that Isla seemed to notice. She had apparently abandoned years of practiced decorum today, completely focused on me as she was.

Really, seeing her this excited was the best wedding present she could have given me.

"You're getting married today!" She squealed uncharacteristically, flouncing herself onto my feather mattress.

My mother laughed and shifted to make room for Isla, though my friend's personality occupied more space than her small frame did. Excited butterflies filled my stomach. Not only would I be Oliver's wife after today, but Isla's cousin in truth. I had longed to call her sister for years now, but cousin was not a bad consolation.

My maid, Clara, beamed as she brought us our breakfast tray. I scarcely got two bites down before I was rushed into the bath and then to my immense vanity.

Isla applied a line of kohl to my eyelids and over my lashes to make my green eyes appear a little larger. She finished up by adding a combination of crushed berries to my full lips and cheeks. The color highlighted my fading freckles.

"Do you have something for these?" I asked Isla, pointing.

"You want to cover your freckles?" She lowered her brows.

"Just for today."

Isla shook her head but obliged, deft hands brushing paint on my face.

Clara was busy pinning the loosened braids of my dark hair up at the base of my neck when my mother approached and placed an unfamiliar tiara on my head.

"I had this crafted for your wedding day," she told me, leading me away from the others to stand in front of my full-length gilded mirror.

I gasped. My closet was full of jewels, but this was something else entirely. My mother smiled at me as I examined the glistening diadem. I could only describe it as silver snow caught in a circlet of jewels. A variety of diamonds rose and fell to form each individual snowflake, and small blue sapphires accentuated the delicate design.

My eyes drifted to my dress. The soft, crushed white velvet of the gorgeous gown hugged the length of my arms and fit nicely against my torso, complimenting my curves before flowing out into a trailing train. The only ornamentation on the dress itself was a simple crystal-studded silver belt that rested across my hips. Whoever had picked out this dress had chosen well.

I look like a Winter Faerie Queen.

When I turned back to my mother to thank her, the grave expression on her graceful features gave me pause.

"Listen, Charlotte…" She hesitated.

Unbridled horror flooded my veins. *Is she actually going to have this talk now, with my suites full of people?*

Besides, she was a few years late to this discussion. My governess had long since explained the mechanics of things to me. I didn't want to go through such a conversation once more with my mother, let alone in front of a room full of servants.

Fortunately, before she could piece together whatever she was going to say, a solid booming noise made us both jump. She smiled and went to answer the door.

"Is she ready, Elspeth?" My father's voice wasn't much softer than the knock had been.

"She is," my mother replied.

I admired the sight of them for a moment before stepping into the hallway as well. His towering form dwarfed my mother's petite one, and her sepia complexion made his own ivory tone even fairer by comparison. The contrast was beautiful.

My father cleared his throat and swallowed a couple of times as he shifted his weight back and forth, staring at me with a smile in his eyes. Wordlessly, he held out an arm and nodded to the hallway. I beamed at him. His features were severe and his manner gruff, but he had never given me reason to doubt his love.

Mother and Isla hurried ahead to take their seats, though the latter seemed to walk deliberately slow when she passed my brother. Finnian was waiting in the hallway, ready to walk at my other side. He had my mother's darker skin, but his amber-colored eyes and sharp features were purely my father's. His openly warm expression was all his own, and it turned warmer still as he took in the sight of my best friend.

From the emerald gown that matched her eyes, to the golden circlet woven into her intensely crimson hair, I could hardly blame him for staring. My mother indulged them for half a second before shooing her along, leaving me alone with my father and brother.

This is it.

I walked at a stately pace toward the Grand Hall, arms linked with the two most important men in my life, after

Oli. Their steadying presences helped to still my frazzled nerves. My whole life was about to change.

We were only a few feet from the entrance to the Grand Hall when Captain Brodie approached on hastened footsteps, alarm in his features.

"King Brannan—" The Captain stopped with a glance in my direction.

The butterflies in my stomach beat furiously, but this time, it didn't feel like excitement. I felt the blood drain from my face. Though I hadn't noticed it before, the cold of winter penetrated to my bones and a shiver ran up my spine. A lump formed in the pit of my stomach as I took in Brodie's demeanor: sweat on the brow, eyes that wouldn't meet mine, a slight downward hunch to his shoulders...

He never hesitates to speak in front of me. Something is wrong.

"Out with it, Captain," my father commanded, impatience clipping his words.

"Of course, Sire." Brodie resolutely avoided my probing gaze. "It's Prince Oliver. He has been taken."

CHAPTER 3

I was freezing, and the snow was falling faster.

How long have I been out here?

I made it nearly all the way to the sanctuary of my favorite willow tree before I tripped over the voluminous skirts of my gown. Once I was on the ground, I found I had little desire to rise. My guards moved to help me up, but I ordered them away. They eventually retreated, leaving me more or less alone.

Which was what I wanted. *Right?*

Oli is gone. Has he been hurt? What about the treaty?

I felt panic rise in my chest once again. I still struggled to steady my heartbeat when the sound of even footsteps approached.

"I told you to leave me."

A throat cleared behind me. Even though he hadn't said anything else, I would know that voice anywhere.

Stars, anyone but him.

"Now is hardly the time for your judgment, Logan.

Feel free to be elsewhere." I didn't bother to turn as I addressed Oliver's half-brother. It was still more courtesy than he generally afforded me, so I braced myself for his scathing response.

Instead, silence settled over us, thicker than the snow on the ground. I finally glanced over my shoulder at him, raising an eyebrow.

His expression was unreadable, even with his scarlet hair pulled away from his face, but I could feel the disapproval emanating from him like venomous snakes poised to strike the moment they found a weakness.

I turned away. If he had nothing to say, then neither did I. Besides, it took all my energy to combat the chill that was permeating every inch of my being. Shivers wracked my body, and my hands turned from red to a pale shade of blue.

Still, we said nothing. At least I was numb now, from the inside out. Though I wasn't convinced the glacial temperatures were responsible for all of that.

"Will ye be walking back on your own, or shall I carry ye, Highness?" His voice sounded unnaturally loud in the wake of our unspoken standoff, and even more thickly accented than I remembered.

Logan's mother had been from the outer villages in Luan, and every once in a while, that brogue emerged. Not that it in any way hindered the authority in his voice. Or the condescension, for that matter.

My panic was being overtaken by fury with each moment he stood there. I shot him a glare he didn't deign to acknowledge before clumsily getting to my feet amidst the snow tumbling off my dress.

He gestured gallantly for me to lead the way. I took several steps, or rather, hobbled. My bare foot had gone numb from its contact with the icy ground.

Logan watched me struggle without bothering to feign patience. After his third audible sigh, he leaned in to pick me up.

"Don't even think about—" I stepped away and simultaneously raised a shivering hand to stop him.

He acted for all the world as though I had neither spoken, nor moved. I could have been a statue for all the emotion on his face as he scooped me into his arms and walked steadily toward the castle without so much as a word.

"Put. Me. Down."

No response.

I scowled at him.

"This is ridiculous and humiliating."

Still nothing. Only his clenched jaw gave away any emotion at all. He was irritated.

Good. So was I.

"I can walk, Logan!" I tried again, but my chattering teeth detracted from the ire I was attempting to convey.

I'd never admit that part of me was grateful not to make the trek back on my frozen foot. Of course, another part of me hoped he pulled a muscle from the strain of carrying me.

I was hardly petite. Between my height and curvy

frame, I had never been what one would consider dainty. I was far too cold to be self-conscious, though.

Just as I had accepted we would make the rest of the undignified trek in silence, he finally spoke.

"… incredibly selfish." The words were quiet, barely more than a whisper.

"Excuse me?" I asked incredulously.

He hesitated for only a moment before continuing his scolding.

"All of Castle Chridhe is in an uproar looking for leads and making plans for what to do next, and what were you doing, Princess? Pouting and forcing your guards to freeze to death."

I was too shocked to even respond. This went beyond even Logan's typical behavior. I knew he didn't care for me and hadn't for some time, but this was uncalled for. Not to mention the arrogant arse had clearly sent my guards away without so much as consulting me.

"How dare you." I hissed the words through clenched teeth.

"Ach! Of course, Highness." He had refused to call me by anything but my title for the past three years. "How dare I even consider assaulting ye with somethin' so trivial as the truth."

I jerked away from him, forcing him to put me down. I may have also stomped on his foot as I hit the ground. He was upset about his brother, I knew, but I had just lost my husband.

Storming away from him, I limped the rest of the way back to the castle.

There was a time Logan would never have raised his voice to me. To anyone, really. He had been downright congenial when I met him, but his appointment to Captain of Luan's Guard had changed that. I hoped my brother would retain his own kind nature when his appointment became official.

The life of a princess did not lend itself to many friends. The few my age at court were either wary of being too close to me or desperate to win my favor for reasons that had nothing to do with companionship.

I had spent most of every day alone in lessons with my tutors for as long as I could remember. The only respite from that schedule had been the three weeks of the year I spent in Luan, and the three weeks Oli and Logan would come here.

I didn't know if I could handle losing another friend, let alone my brother.

The guards heaved opened the massive wooden doors for me, and I made my way toward the war room. If the monarchs were meeting already, to plan the next steps, that was where they would be.

I cursed under my breath as Logan fumed past me, easily outpacing my hobbled gait. He stomped into the war room and let the door slam behind him with a bang.

Bastard.

My mother found me just before I entered the meeting and motioned me toward the small alcove directly across from it. Worry lined her face.

"Mother, I'm..." I didn't know how I was going to

finish that sentence, but I didn't need to. She reached out for my hand, placing it in both of hers.

The small gesture threatened to break my resolve. If my anger disappeared, I would be nothing but raw emotions again. A tear slipped down my cheek, and I looked away from her. I didn't know what she was thinking, but I couldn't bear it if she displayed a hint of pity.

My mother gently tilted my chin to face her and spoke in a clear, even voice. There was no trace of pity or sadness. Instead, I saw the Queen in her.

Strong. Determined. Wise.

"Darling, I know you are overwhelmed with sadness and worry. But all is not lost. Not yet. If anyone can bring Oliver back, it will be our armies. They would climb the Masach Mountains for you, my child, to bring home the man you love."

The man I love. Who is gone. Panic surged once more through my veins.

She must have noticed. "Charlotte, they wouldn't have taken Oliver away if they wished the worst for him."

She means death. My mind snagged on the word that my mother refused to say. I forced myself to focus on what she had said. And she was right.

This isn't over yet.

Taking a deep breath, I left the alcove and nodded to the sentries to open the doors to the war room. As an afterthought, I slipped off my other shoe and straightened my crown. I was disheveled and barefoot, but I would be damned if that kept me from doing everything I could to help Oliver.

CHAPTER 4

The room was suffocating, the air thick with tension rolling off the powerful men standing so close together. Despite the urgency of the situation, nothing was getting done. Everyone crowded around the imposing circular table in the center of the space, studying a detailed map of my kingdom. Small flags littered the parchment. Black represented where the rebels had recently been active, and blue and silver represented where our men would be sent.

The kingdoms had differing opinions on where the search parties should begin, the most vocal disagreement between Brodie and Earc. The thundering shouts were exacerbating my pounding head and doing nothing to move the plans for action forward.

Even our poor servants looked as if they were trying to disappear into the tapestries on the walls, none daring to risk drawing the attention of the enraged leaders.

Everyone around me completely avoided looking in

my direction, my sorry state just one more reminder of how differently the day had gone from what we had all expected.

Half of the circular table was comprised of my entire family and Captain Brodie. On the other side were Logan, his father, the King of Luan, and his uncle, Laird Earc. Queen Siobhan paced back and forth behind the men, her fury and concern for her son apparent in every line of her elegant features.

My mind took me back to a long-forgotten memory. Looking around the room, I imagined for a moment that Oli was here. We were hiding from my governess under this very table, muffling our giggles, hoping no one would find us. His small hand held mine as we watched her scurry from the war room, clearly exasperated with us. I had started to feel guilty and went to call out for her when Oli leaned over and gave me a light peck on the cheek. *My very first kiss.*

I shook off the memory and felt his absence like a stab in my chest.

"Logan will, of course, lead a retinue of our kingsmen." King Rowan gestured to his eldest son. "He will have the best chance at bringing his brother home."

Luan's Captain inclined his head respectfully in his father's direction.

"There is no need for H'Ria's kingsmen to become further involved," Earc said to my father and Captain Brodie, removing a grouping of flags from the map.

"Don't you mean *our* kingsmen? Or have you forgotten that the elite knights are soon to be a combined force for all of Lochlann? We would have been united today," the Captain responded angrily. "This happened here in H'Ria, so we most certainly will be involved in the search!" He slammed the blue markers back in place.

"That is the issue, is it not? My nephew was kidnapped in your kingdom, on your watch, with your men keeping guard! And now, we find that one of King Brannan's own servants is missing as well." Earc's dark eyes narrowed in accusation.

My hand went to my mouth. *What? What servant?* This was news to me. If Oli had been here, he would have had no problem voicing the question. My throat tightened, and I forced myself to focus.

"We are looking into that," Brodie said, his muscles tense. He spoke with controlled anger. "We have no idea if the incidents are even related. Once we had all of the *facts,* we intended to share them with you."

"Facts? You should be sharing all information with us. Your king is not the only king here, and my brother deserves more respect than you are showing him," Earc spat back.

The vehement back and forth was getting out of hand, and I couldn't listen anymore. I had been here only moments, but my temples were already throbbing, my blood rushing with the need to do something, anything other than sit here and argue. Apparently, my father felt the same.

"Enough!" The ferocity in the King of H'Ria's voice was enough to silence everyone at once. "Both sides will be sending men to find the prince." My father looked to

Luan's King when speaking, ignoring Laird Earc's protest. "My men have extensive knowledge of the land and a vested interest in retrieving their future sovereign. Your men, I am sure, are eager to ensure the safety of their beloved prince. There is no reason we cannot work together with men from both countries in each contingent."

Earc started to speak again before the sight of King Brannan's cold expression silenced him. My father cleared his throat and continued as if the interruption never happened.

"I am sure Your Majesties will not wish to remain without guards of your own, so a few kingsmen will remain here, offering protection for the royal families. And this way, we can ensure there is sufficient manpower to combat any rebels our soldiers encounter."

Studying the map for a moment, he moved the blue and silver flags to three separate places.

"We will send out three parties. Our kingsmen will head directly west. This is where the Aramach have caused the most trouble recently. We will send word to our men in Bala to assist in the search. Another contingent will head north, searching and questioning the lairds and villages nearest the castle. The last will head east toward Rionn."

I bit my lip. Everyone knew the rebels were to the west and south. The country of Rionn was staunchly neutral and guarded their borders fiercely. They would never allow the Aramach to cross, least of all with a political prisoner.

Is he really going to waste our resources just to placate the Luanians?

I looked around the room to see if anyone else would object. Logan was glaring at me. No surprise there. My mother's face was almost too passive. She saw the same issues I did. I opened my mouth, then closed it. My father would not welcome my dissension.

He looked at King Rowan and asked him directly. "Is this acceptable to you?"

Rowan was an older, more hardened version of Logan. His features, like his eldest son's, rarely revealed what he was thinking. Raising his crimson eyebrows for a moment, he deliberated before finally nodding.

"It is."

"And just who will you trust to lead this retinue?" Queen Siobhan spoke in her usual haughty tone. She clearly had no reservations in speaking during the war council. "Not this half-soldier, I presume," she spat.

Brodie's face turned an alarming shade of purple as he stared down the Queen. It was true that he had lost a hand in the war, but he was a brilliant strategist. I felt the heat of my anger rise in my cheeks at the insult. My mother's features went tight with offense. Even Logan's jaw clenched as he stared at his step-mother. But my father simply glared at Luan's monarchy in disbelief before correcting its Queen.

"Brodie is an unparalleled warrior who does not deserve your scorn." He gritted the words out through clenched teeth. "His services, however, are required here. Prince Finnian will be the one to lead our retinue. They

31

will be the ones to take our men west. Is that acceptable?" My father formed this as a question, but his tone implied it was his command.

Queen Siobhan stiffened at the implication before looking somewhat mollified as she studied my brother with a practiced eye. Finally, she nodded. They may not be overly familiar with our Captain of the Guard, but they did know Finn. And maybe it said something of what my father felt about this rescue mission that he was willing to send his son into danger.

"Then it is decided," my father said. "We will tell the men to prepare to leave at once. We have lost enough time as it is."

The deafening sound of the door slamming open jolted my awareness. Earc had not taken kindly to being ignored. Everyone else was spilling out into the hall, eager to get started with the search.

They were leaving to find Oli. That should have been good news, but the churning in my gut refused to abate. The strain in the room reminded me too much of what was at stake — not only Oliver's life, but the fate of our kingdoms.

The long war had nearly destroyed Luan and H'Ria both. The treaty that decided my fate, my marriage to Oli, was threatening to dissolve into nothing. If we didn't find him, would we be facing war again, even after eighteen years of tentative peace?

I headed back to my chambers to find Isla waiting for me. The normally implacable girl had tears in her eyes.

"Oli?" Her voice was shaky.

I shook my head. "He's gone. Logan and Finn are leading a company to go after him."

"So, we just wait for news, then?"

There it was again. That violent feeling in my gut. They would go after my betrothed, a man who should have been my husband by now, and I would stay here. Useless.

CHAPTER 5

I raced to my chamber pot and emptied every last morsel from my stomach. Isla came beside me to place her hand on my tiara, stopping it from tumbling into the ceramic basin. She handed me a cloth with shaking hands, and I wiped my face.

She sank down next to me against the cold stone. My wedding gown was no longer pristine after my fall outside, so what did it matter if I sat on the floor next to my chamber pot?

Oliver was gone. Our kingdoms were once again at each other's throats. And I was supposed to simply wait. The thoughts kept repeating in my mind, but they felt wrong every time.

Eventually, Isla and I rose from the floor to sit in the chairs next to the hearth. The warmth attempted to ease some of the tension in my muscles, but it couldn't quite thaw the anxiety I felt for Oliver, or this plan where I sat aside and did nothing.

Just as I settled into the cushions, Clara entered with a tea tray and my missing shoe.

With trembling fingers, she placed a shaking cup and saucer into Isla's hands, nearly spilling it everywhere. I caught Isla's confused expression before my own cup went clashing to the floor.

"I'm so sorry, Highness!" Clara cried as she bent over to pick up the broken pieces.

Looking down at her in shock, I reached out and pulled her hands into mine. Clara was young, barely older than me, but I had never known her to be nervous. Something was bothering her.

"Clara, is something the matter?"

"Oh, Highness!" She looked up with regret written all over her features. "I'm so sorry. I should've told you sooner."

"Told me what?" My brows furrowed.

"I just didn't know what it meant at the time." She pulled her hands back, looking away.

"Clara…" I said her name gently to encourage her to speak.

"I overheard them talking, and I didn't know what it meant."

She wasn't making any sense. I looked up at Isla to find the same foreboding on her face that stirred within me.

"Start from the beginning, Clara," Isla said calmly.

"There were soldiers, one H'Rian and one Luanian, in the servants' stairwell. That's not unusual, the servants and the soldiers." Clara blushed before continuing. "But

36

they spoke of the wedding day, and 'making sure they got them out without incident,' and they scattered when I came near. I thought they were only talking of sneaking in to see the courtesans until I heard about your prince and Fergus."

"Fergus?" I asked.

"He was the servant assigned to Prince Oliver, Your Highness."

I exchanged another look with my best friend.

"Where are the soldiers now, Clara?" Isla asked. "Could you point them out if you saw them?"

Clara shook her head, and my heart sank. But she wasn't finished.

"They are not here, Milady. They were kingsmen. Their group left nearly an hour ago with Captain Logan and His Highness."

Logan and Finn were both in danger. Not to mention the mission to find Oli.

"Thank you, Clara." I said the words with more calm than I felt. "Speak of this to no one else for the time being."

"Of course, Princess." She nodded steadier this time and left the room.

How did a disorganized, ragtag band of rebels manage to infiltrate the armies of both kingdoms? I looked to Isla, that heaving feeling returning to my stomach.

"What do you want to do, Charlie?" Isla stared at me wide-eyed, wringing her hands until her knuckles turned white.

"I don't know."

"Think about it, Charlie. What does your gut tell you?" She paced the room, gathering her hair to one side and running her fingers through it over and over.

My mind reeled. If there were traitors among the kingsmen, then maybe there were others. *Who can we trust?*

We could tell my father, but he would be in the same dilemma. Or if both sides knew, would they imagine that the other was plotting against them? I had thought the unfulfilled treaty was the biggest threat to war, but this could be the breaking point.

I massaged my temples, my mind racing through every possibility. What did I want to do? What could we do?

"Someone has to warn them, but there isn't anyone we can trust." My nausea began to fade as the plan took shape in my mind.

"Then how?" Isla stopped pacing.

How, indeed. Logan and Finn could be in danger. Oli was in actual danger. What would become of our makeshift family by the time this was all over?

Can I truly do this? Fifteen years of training to rule as future Queen told me the answer was no. That I should stay in the castle where I was safe, helping to ease the tensions of our people with my mere presence. That I had no business gallivanting off to do a man's work.

But there was another part of me, smaller, buried — but no less real — saying: *If not me, then who?*

"I know that face." Hope shone from Isla's eyes. "I haven't seen that look in years, but I know that face. Tell me what you're plotting."

"I'm not sure yet. Maybe nothing. My father would kill me."

Isla's lips tightened in determination. She got to her knees and took both of my hands in hers, piercing me with an unwavering gaze.

"Charlie, I know as well as anyone what's expected of you. But just this once, I'm going to ask you: What do *you* think we should do?"

I paused before answering, working out the last of the details in my mind until I was certain there was no other option. A hesitant smile crept onto my lips as I returned her look.

"I have a plan."

CHAPTER 6

"I still can't believe *this* was your plan," Isla grumbled at me again. Her face was nearly as red as her hair while Clara helped her wrestle into yet another set of armor. Hopefully, this one would be small enough for her to manage.

Isla's comment was a fair one.

When I initially imagined disguising ourselves as soldiers to go warn Finn and Logan, then sneaking into the squadron that had set off to find Oli, it never occurred to me that putting on armor would be so blasted complicated.

Standing in this room, it was hard not to be assaulted by memories. How many times had I watched Oli sparring in this space? Closing my eyes, I could almost feel him. The way he would laugh as he scooped me up in sweaty arms, spinning me around. The way I would pretend to be disgusted, but secretly relished every chance to be that close to him.

I opened my eyes, my resolve hardening in the wake of the memory. I held my hand out for the bandage Clara had brought for me to bind my chest, the most identifying mark of me being a woman. This may not be a perfect plan, but it was what we had.

Once Clara had told us about the conversation she'd heard, we knew we didn't have a choice. We needed to warn my brother and Logan. Isla grappled clumsily with another set of armor.

"I can't even reach the gauntlets!" she whisper-yelled. This was the fourth set of armor she'd tried.

I cocked my head and considered her. "Maybe you could... hold the reins in your elbows?"

Her stormy expression morphed into one of mirth, and she laughed a little too loudly. Unexpected laughter bubbled up in my chest as well, though I tried to stifle it. Not only did we need to be quiet, but how could we laugh when the people we loved were in danger?

Then again, whatever it takes to keep us moving forward.

The words on my family crest rang loudly in my mind. *Tellus Amat Fortis.* The World Loves the Strong Ones. If laughing was what kept us that way, then so be it.

However, it still might get us caught.

"Shh," I whispered, trying to add a bit of sternness to my tone.

Though I was the heir to the throne, my father would certainly wonder what we were doing if I was discovered here.

A thought struck me. I was only the heir if we found Oliver. If we didn't find him, I really wasn't sure what that would mean for H'Ria. The throne had never been passed down to a female alone.

I fiddled with the necklace that held my wedding ring. Marrying anyone but Oliver was unimaginable. Unthinkable.

I shook the thought away. *One problem at a time.*

Because of the day's events, I had convinced my parents that I was retiring early. In reality, Clara and Isla had waited for the guard shift to change and snuck into the armory to find a disguise while I went to secure some men's clothing for us to wear underneath.

I hadn't loved the idea of wearing the heavy armor, but we would need a disguise that would keep us safe in order to make it to the men. Two women traveling alone would never escape notice. The armor would tell passersby that we were knights on a mission for the crown, and that we could defend ourselves.

Our plan had slowly evolved from there. It wasn't foolproof, but we had no more time to figure out something better. We would just have to make it work. I tried not to think about the very real danger lurking outside of these walls.

The truth was, the threat had gotten inside the walls as well. There was no escaping it now, only facing it, head on.

To that end, Clara would help us sneak past the guards tonight. In the morning, she would deliver the letter I'd written explaining everything to my mother. I could only hope we would be well away by then.

We finally got Isla into her armor, then we moved on

to finagling mine. It hadn't been an issue finding armor to fit my larger frame, but we quickly discovered a different sort of problem.

"I can't just squash them down, Isla," I said.

"Who knew there were downsides to having large breasts," my friend jibed, causing Clara to snicker under her breath.

"Shhhh! We can't get caught because of my bosoms," I said, inciting yet another round of hushed laughter, though I had been serious. The adrenaline from our worry and the sneaking around was making us all a bit too giddy.

"The other armor clanks against your torso too much. You need…" Isla looked around until her eyes landed on a stack of spare pillows. She grabbed one and stuffed it in front of my stomach to help support the space needed for my chest.

"Yes, I think this will work. Are you ready?" I handed Isla the broadsword Clara had found for us. I was impatient to get out of the castle walls and on our way.

"Sure," she said with her typical dark sarcasm. "As ready as I think a Duchess can be in hand-me-down armor that smells like sweat and halitosis."

CHAPTER 7

I was beginning to believe I had not properly thought this plan through, and it wasn't yet dawn.

The bulky armor chafed against my skin through my underclothes, but we didn't want to slow our pace, knowing that traitorous soldiers could be riding alongside my brother. The pillow Isla had stuffed under the midsection of my armor helped with the abrasive armor, but only added to the insular effect of my multiple layers of clothing.

My friend didn't seem to be faring much better. Isla shifted in discomfort, huffing under her breath.

"How is it even possible to sweat in these temperatures?" she grumbled, finally removing her helmet.

I tried to look over at her and laugh, but my helmet wouldn't allow it. "Let's focus on something else. Distract me from all this sweating and constant worry," I said, removing my own confining helmet and taking a large swill of my canteen. The cold water was refreshing after being overheated for so long, and the icy breeze was a welcome relief as perspiration rolled down my neck.

I glanced around us, able to see clearly without the obstruction of my visor. Glistening snow covered the earth, masking the world in beauty. Winter had always been my favorite season. Everything just felt magical when it snowed.

Isla's voice pulled me from my thoughts. "My betrothal to the Socairan Duke was confirmed shortly before we left the castle." She delivered the words without inflection.

A number of responses died in my throat. I was unsure of what to say. I knew she wouldn't want my pity; that wasn't Isla's way. But this news was devastating. Socair was on the other side of the Masach Mountains. How would she cope so far from family and friends? How would we see each other? That wasn't even the worst part, though.

"It's all right, Charlie." How like her to comfort me when it should have been the other way around. "It is what it is. You know my mother will not be swayed on this matter. We've both known that for a long time now."

The few times I had met Isla's mother, it had been immediately evident she was unwell. She kept to her rooms the majority of the time. When she did emerge, it was with a distant, mournful expression.

"Did she say why?" I asked.

Isla sighed before responding. "She alleges ties to Socair would be advantageous, though I suspect her true motivation lies closer to ensuring my everlasting misery."

Her lips twisted in a sour expression as she narrowed her eyes straight ahead, staring down the world before her.

I didn't know enough about the woman to know whether that was fair.

"Have you told Finn?"

She was silent for a moment, and I almost regretted asking. I didn't want to cause her any more pain.

"No." Her voice was barely above a whisper.

I didn't push her for more of an explanation. This news would devastate my brother as much as it clearly had Isla. I wondered at her earlier comment regarding her mother's motives. A duke in Socair was nowhere near the match Finn would have been, even taking affection out of the equation. But the prejudices ran deep in our kingdoms, despite the years of peace, and Isla's mother had more reason to feel that way than most.

Isla's father had died three years after the war ended. The injuries he sustained during battle had left him weakened when he returned home, and her mother had never forgiven my kingdom for the devastating loss.

Will we never stop paying for our parents' war?

"I'm sorry, Isla. Truly. I wish there were something I could do—" I started.

"It's all right, Charlie. There's nothing to be done. It's the way of our world to sell our women into alliances as if they were cattle to be traded." She chuckled, but I knew it was a humorless gesture. "It happened to you, it's happening to me, and it will happen to scores of women after us. Besides, maybe the rumors are wrong and it will turn out like what you and Oli have."

47

"Yeah, you're right. Maybe it will be great." I gave her a tight smile, wanting to believe the words.

At the mention of his name, I couldn't help but be pulled back into my own despair for a moment.

"Do you think Oli is—?" I stopped myself before I could finish the question. I wasn't even sure what I wanted to ask, let alone hear the answer.

She took a deep, fortifying breath before answering. "I really hope so. It seems likely that if they had wanted him…" She paused, then picked up in a stronger tone. "If they had wanted him dead, they wouldn't have gone to the trouble of taking him."

I nodded. It was the same conclusion my mother had drawn.

"The question is, 'why?'" Isla said.

I had been pondering that very thing most of the ride thus far. "Ultimately," I said, "the Aramach want an end to the monarchy, so it makes sense that they would do their utmost to disrupt a treaty that would strengthen two kingdoms."

"So then, it's left to wonder, why not just kill him?" She blanched at her own blunt words. "Don't mistake me. I'm grateful. But that would be the surest way to end the alliance."

I nibbled at the inside of my cheek, turning her words over in my head. The rebels were hardly held back by a sense of morality, from what I'd heard. And then there was still the conundrum of having soldiers from both kingdoms involved.

What are we missing?

"Do you think Rionn could be involved?" Isla's tone was thoughtful. "I know they profess to be neutral, but they can't be too happy with the two monarchies they share a border with uniting."

I shrugged. "That's quite a leap to make when we have no basis for it, but I suppose we shouldn't rule it out."

We were both silent a moment while I held back the real question lingering on my lips.

Are they hurting him?

The sound of our horses' hooves on the road and the sight of the gently falling snowflakes lulled us into our own melancholy thoughts for a time.

I desperately tried to think of something happier. The year I turned seven, Finn and I made our first annual visit to the Luanian castle. My younger brother held my hand as I nervously beheld my future husband for the first time. Even as a child, Oli had been beautiful. He was quick to smile, his dark hair always falling into his blue eyes while he plotted some new mischief. He had been exactly the kind of boy I could picture marrying someday. The three of us quickly became inseparable.

By the following year, Logan had arrived, and Isla shortly after. Those years were the happiest of my life. The five of us formed our own perfect family, and the weeks we were together were nothing short of magical. When we had to go our separate ways, we made avid use of the messenger birds, anxiously awaiting updates from each of our friends.

Then, of course, Logan became Captain of the Guard, and also an arsehole. Isla had never been able to come to

Chridhe, but Logan had eventually stopped coming also. Then Finn became so occupied with his own training duties that, by the winter I turned sixteen, everything had changed.

I sighed.

So much for happier memories.

CHAPTER 8

I sla continued to look as morose as I felt. We needed a shift in focus to keep us going. So, I blurted out the first thing that came to mind.

"I need to take a piss." I spoke in the deepest voice I could muster.

Isla sputtered, releasing a choked sort of laughter. "What did you just say?" Her voice was even more proper than usual, as if to make up for my crassness.

"I just thought we should practice speaking like the soldiers."

Her armor clanked with the shaking of her shoulders.

"And I really do," I added.

"And just how do you propose we do that?" She gestured to the armor we were stuck in and the empty moors around us. "So much for your brilliant plan."

Admittedly, I hadn't considered how we would take care of those needs. "Well, feel free to contribute at any time." I leveled her with a look. Heavy snowflakes settled onto my eyelashes, likely ruining the effect.

"Very well," she said, squinting into the cold. "We hide behind a— something. And be about our business as quickly as possible."

"Yes, thank you. That was helpful," I replied sarcastically, earning an eye roll from her.

I scanned the vast rolling hills and sparse bushes of the countryside on either side of the main road, then back to Isla. There was a rather large hill ahead, obscuring the rest of the path, that likely offered similar options. She must have come to the same conclusion. We looked at each other and laughed, only intensifying my mounting need for a privy.

"Let's just go over here. We can hide behind that hill and let the horses shield us," I offered.

She nodded, and we led the horses off the path. There, we were presented with a new problem. It had been trouble enough getting on the horse. I hadn't the slightest notion how to dismount in this bulky armor.

"After you," I said to Isla, gesturing to the snowy grass below.

There was a stilted, proud silence. "I can't," she said.

The laughter I had been holding at bay spilled out again. I moved to swing my stiff leg over my horse. My heel must have caught on the saddle, and I proceeded to fall the rest of the way to the ground, one leg still stuck in the stirrups.

I gasped as the air left my lungs and stars momentarily spotted my vision.

I was suddenly grateful for the war destriers we'd decided to take. Not only could they handle the added weight of the armor, but they didn't seem even slightly bothered by my bumbling fall. Whereas my portly mare would have most definitely been spooked and ended up running away, dragging me behind her.

I continued to lay on the ground, trying to catch my breath while Isla mocked me from her saddle.

"We're terrible soldiers," she remarked.

I couldn't help but agree. Slowly and awkwardly, I made my way back to my feet. "I should just let you fall, too," I said, leaning on my horse for support.

"You wouldn't." She quirked an eyebrow.

"Try me."

"Ok, I'll stop. Promise. Just help me down. Please?" Her serious expression was morphing into a mirthful grin before she could help herself.

I shook my head but held my arms out to catch her. We managed to both stay upright while she tumbled gracelessly from her horse.

We stared dubiously at our makeshift privy for a moment. Isla hesitated another beat before setting to work on her armor. I sighed and reluctantly followed suit.

I was just shimmying back into my pilfered breeches when the sound of hoofbeats reached our ears. I grabbed Isla's arm in surprise, causing her to stumble bare-arsed into the snow. Her mouth dropped open in shock. I held my hand over my lips to muffle my cackling.

"Good mornin'! Be ye needin' any help, sirs?"

Isla and I exchanged alarmed glances before I attempted to speak.

"Ach! Nay, my good man." *What am I saying?*

"Deeper!" Isla hissed at me to lower the octave of my voice.

"No, thank ye," I said. *Ye?* "My companion is just a wee bit sick."

"You sound ridiculous. And like you're making fun of him," Isla whispered.

"Well, how do the men talk?" I asked quietly.

"I 'eard ye from the road," the man called. "And I was wantin' ta be sure there weren't any trouble is all. Will ye be goin' along with the rest o' them soldiers o'er the inn?"

I stumbled a little. *The rest of them? Did that mean we were close?*

"Aye. We were about to meet them posthaste."

"Posthaste? Stars, Charlie!" Isla mumbled.

"Shush, woman! I don't see you helping!" I snapped back at her at the same low volume.

"I'm sick, remember?" She gave a loud groan to play into the façade.

Suspicion was evident on the man's features, even from here, but he didn't make any remarks about the unfortunate show he was witnessing.

"Aye. Well, good luck then!" he said at last, shaking his head and turning his horse back to the road.

"My arse is frozen!" Isla exclaimed as soon as he was out of earshot.

"I'm sorry for your arse, but, Isla, did you hear what he said?"

She shot me a dirty look and shook her head.

I smiled widely. "We've finally caught up to the men."

CHAPTER 9

"Do you know what else it means?" Isla said sardonically. "We didn't have to use those hills as a privy."

We stared at the roads and buildings in front of us. They had, in fact, been lying just beyond that large hill. After putting our helmets back on, we continued into the village. This time, we were walking our horses, as we'd lacked the ability to wrestle our sore and exhausted bodies back on top of them.

"Well, I guess the other option would've been dismounting in front of all those people," I said.

We glanced at each other and shook our heads. Decidedly, we had made the right choice.

Despite the early hour, people were busy opening their shops and preparing their wagons to sell various wares. The lands east of the Condie River had remained prosperous, untouched by war, while those farther west had spent the past eighteen years doing their utmost to rebuild. We were still well east of the river, and it showed in the pristine historic buildings and unhaunted faces of the citizens.

We trudged down the sludge-packed lanes, following the signs for the local inn. That's where the man had said the other soldiers were staying. Hopefully, they hadn't left yet.

"Do you smell that?" Isla inhaled deeply.

"Smell wha…?" The question died on my lips just as the scent hit me.

Our heads jerked toward the intoxicating aroma of spices and roasted meats wafting our way. I swayed on my feet. We hadn't eaten since breakfast the day before. The memory assaulted me with a visceral wrench to my gut, that fewer than twenty-four hours before, I had hardly been able to contain my elation.

Oli is alive, I reminded myself. *He has to be.* And we had information that could help save him. Stuffing my hunger down for the moment, I pulled Isla away from the enticing aroma, heading instead for the row of clearly-marked taverns. Maybe there would be time to come back later.

Stables peeked out from behind the double-story buildings, but it was impossible to tell from here which one was housing royal mounts or if the soldiers were split between several of the inns.

We would have to enter each stable and look for my brother's or Logan's horse. I tried not to think about how much more time we would lose. Our latrine break had taken far longer than expected, but there was nothing we could do about that now.

Several of the townespeople looked askance at Isla and me as we walked by. I examined her armor and then my own for any obvious issues, but everything seemed to be in order.

Odd.

I couldn't concern myself with that right now, though. We needed to find Finn. I attempted to quicken my lumbering gait to no avail. The hunger and exhaustion had seeped into my bones. I was alternately sweating and shivering, and my limbs were so heavy from managing the added weight of the armor that it was all I could do just to keep walking.

If I was exhausted, I doubted Isla was faring much better. She was tiny, but her armor was no less heavy than mine. Still, she plodded next to me without complaint, our horses trudging alongside us. I was beginning to feel light-headed with fatigue, I didn't even register the sound of my brother's voice until Isla stopped dead in her tracks.

"Lieutenants, what are you doing here?" His authoritative tone behind us sent a surge of pride through my veins. He would make a respectable Captain of the Guard.

"It's Finn!" Isla whispered.

I didn't see the lieutenants to whom he was referring, but we were careful not to turn around. No use drawing attention to ourselves in the middle of the road.

"I know, but we can't approach him here. I was going to speak with him in the inn." My head was beginning to throb. I lifted my heavy arm to rub my temples before remembering there was a helmet there. *Blasted stars.*

Finn's voice rang out behind me again. "Lieutenants, I asked you a question."

"He sounds angry now," Isla muttered with a tiny giggle.

If exhaustion was making me light-headed, it seemed to be making her giddy.

"Shh. We need to get off the main road before he sees us." We were only yards away from the closest stables. I led my horse that way, motioning for Isla to follow when I felt a hand clamp down on my armored forearm.

"Identify yourselves," my younger brother demanded in a quiet tone. He had Isla's arm in his other hand, and a fierce expression on his normally mild features.

I opened my mouth to respond, but Isla preempted me with a loud guffaw. I forced my exhausted foot to kick her leg. Instead of achieving the desired result of her silence, the clang only seemed to make her laugh harder.

My brother's face slackened, and his eyes widened.

"Oh, no. Surely this is a jest, but I would know that laugh anywhere. Isla?" He wrenched her visor up, revealing a pert nose and delicate features so at odds with the helmet framing them.

"If you're here, that can only mean…" Unbridled horror overtook his features as he looked in my direction. "Oh, no. No, no, no. Please don't tell me that's you, Charlie."

I tilted my visor before his hand reached me, peering up at him innocently. He squeezed his eyes shut, as though the sight before him would disappear if he wished it.

"Isla, darling." His eyes opened. "Did you drag my sister across the countryside in the middle of the night?"

Isla's eyes narrowed. "She chose to come, just like I chose to accompany her. Do you have something to say about that, Finnian, *darling?*"

My brother wasn't half as smart as he looked because apparently, he did have something to say about that.

"Did you two make this journey alone?" He looked to our horses. "And what have you done to these poor steeds?"

Before I could answer that, he looked back to our faces and his mouth dropped. "You look dreadful. Have you eaten? Slept? And are you sweating in there? Don't you know it's dangerous to wear so many layers of clothing in this weather?"

I didn't bother trying to respond at that point, and neither did Isla. We both knew once my brother got worked up, there was no reasoning with him. Sure enough, he went on.

"I won't even ask about the armor right now. Or whose swords you brazenly stole!"

"They were spares, and we needed them to complete our disguise," I informed him calmly.

"Oh, your disguise? I assume you're referring to your flawless subterfuge as a fat soldier and his child?"

Isla squeaked indignantly at his comment, but we had more pressing issues. My brother's raised voice was bringing unwanted attention.

"Perhaps we could continue this elsewhere," I suggested.

Finn glared at me but ceded the point and led the way to The Tinker Tavern, where he had apparently been staying.

He handed off our horses to the stable boy with an apology about their state, then motioned us toward the green front door. We followed him up a narrow staircase, whimpering with each step until we finally got to a small, tidy room.

He shut the door, then turned on us.

"Now, which of you would like to tell me what the hell you're doing here?"

CHAPTER 10

My brother turned his back while Isla and I wrestled our aching bodies out of the armor, my stomach pillow hitting the floor with a soft thud. We took turns explaining what Clara had told us. For all that we had rushed to get here, it didn't feel like we had very much to say by the time we were finished.

Two unidentified kingsmen may or may not have been in on whatever happened to Oli.

He stood silently, still facing away. Isla tumbled to the bed in only her shift and breeches, her eyelids drooping before she even lay all the way down.

I sank down next to her on the small mattress, attempting to pull the blanket out from under her.

"I am going to fetch you both something else to wear while I figure out our next course of action."

Finn's statement was met with silence. He looked over his shoulder, brow furrowed until he caught sight of Isla's thinly-clad form. His cheeks, already a dark bronze like my mother's, turned ever so slightly a shade of crimson. Then, his face softened, and he attempted to avert his eyes while pulling the covers over us with a resigned sigh.

"Get some rest, you ridiculous women. We'll discuss this further when I return."

I nodded awkwardly as his footsteps receded before the door closed softly behind him. Moments later, Isla's snores sounded from under a mess of crimson curls while I stared up at the ceiling, sleep eluding my efforts.

Wearing the armor today had reminded me of when I would insist we play Warrior Queen when we were all children. The boys had always obliged me, even Finn. My brother was invariably stuck being my enemy, which generally resulted in him being shoved off a rock or stump of some sort. Isla usually took his side, though she was never pushed off any rocks. Logan was my knight, riding into battle with me.

And Oli, of course, was my king.

Once we had defeated our enemies, Oli would come to sweep me off my feet and twirl me around. He would dramatically declare me the Warrior Queen, daring any to challenge his edict.

I smiled at the memory, letting it be a balm to my frayed nerves. We would get my king back. Reaching up, I clutched Oliver's ring tightly to my chest before surrendering my consciousness entirely.

"I LOVE YOU, CHARLIE." I WANTED TO LINGER IN THIS moment forever. Oliver and I were getting married today.

"I love you, too," I tried to say back, but my words were sluggish. I tried again, but my tongue was too heavy in my mouth and my lips refused to move. Suddenly, the room went dark, and I felt Oli being ripped away from me, pulled away down an impossibly long, dark hallway. I tried to scream his name, but only rasping sounds came out.

"Charlie!"

The loud, steady rhythm of marching feet pounded in my eardrums. We were now standing in the middle of a field, completely surrounded by our approaching armies, both H'Ria and Luan. Their swords were drawn, dripping with fresh blood and they were marching toward us.

The perfectly synchronized steps seemed to be forming words. "War. War," the steps said, "War."

It was starting all over again. The smell of death was everywhere, permeating the air around me.

My armies parted briefly, and I could see Oli fighting several knights off him while Luan continued their march toward me. I tried to move, to help Oliver. They were hurting him, but my feet were stuck to the muddy ground beneath me and my voice stopped working all together.

"Charlie!"

My heart thundered as I looked down to see my body slowly turning to stone. I was immobile, and now I was struggling to even breathe.

"Charlie!"

An abrupt slap to my face woke me up from the nightmare I'd been having.

"Stars, Charlie, are you all right? I've been saying your name for the past few minutes." Isla's brow furrowed in concern as she stared down at me.

"What? Where are we? Where's Oli?" Even as I asked, it all came rushing back when I looked up at my friend, half naked and wrapped in a blanket. Oliver was gone, in danger, and today was not my wedding day.

I felt the sadness and worry of the day before washing over me again.

"Charlie?"

"I'm fine," I said half-heartedly, shaking the emotions off. "It was just a bad dream."

They wouldn't have taken Oliver away if they wished the worst for him. My mother and Isla were right. Right now was the time to focus on solutions, not dwell on everything that might go wrong.

I was about to say more when a loud growl sounded from my stomach. Isla was already gulping down too large bites of stew, a second bowl only inches from hers.

Desperately hungry and grateful that I had an excuse not to speak, I inhaled the small portion of stew I assumed was for me, using a piece of hard bread as my spoon.

"Finn brought these a few minutes ago," Isla said, holding up her bowl. "He also brought those." Isla pointed to the tunics, trousers, and buff coats lying on the chair across the room. "He'll be back soon. We need to get dressed, because the men are leaving."

"Does that mean we're going with them? We're going to find Oli?" The possibility that I would actually be able to do something, *anything*, to bring Oliver home had me beaming with hope.

Finn barged back into our room.

"No. That is definitely not what it means."

CHAPTER 11

M y brother shut the door behind him. "You both need to get dressed now. We have to move. We finally have a lead and are leaving as soon as you get your arses in those clothes." He picked up our new clothes and tossed them to us.

Isla snatched up the garments with a frown. Her blanket fell, revealing her scantily-clad form.

"Are those my underwear?" Finn's face reddened as he quickly turned away.

A snort escaped me. "How did you not notice them earlier?"

"I was trying not to look." My brother looked scandalized.

"What's wrong with what we were wearing before?" Isla quickly asked, trying to change the subject. My friend's cheeks matched the red of her hair, but something in her smile told me she was enjoying the revelation of her clothing's original owner.

"Too many things to mention now," Finn said, "but the fact they look nothing like what the rest of the men are wearing is a big one. Armor is for battle, Charlie. Not a search party."

That explained why he hadn't been wearing any yesterday.

"You need to blend in," he continued, tossing a pair of blue wool cloaks at us. "At least, as much as you can without actual uniforms. Then, we can decide who to trust to return you home. And whatever you do, stay far away from Logan. Tensions between our kingdoms are high enough without him insisting I take you two home and continuing on his own to find his brother as he has wanted to do from the outset."

Logan and Finn were friends, but it made sense that the former had wanted a smaller, faster group. Waiting on a unit this size was probably driving him insane.

My brother continued after a short pause. "But make no mistake about it. The moment I am able to work it out safely, the two of you will be heading directly back to the castle." His voice was as authoritative as it had been when he believed we were lieutenants.

"You will be doing no such thing, *little* brother! I made it this far, and I will not go home to simply wait. To be so... *useless*." My voice cracked on the last word, but fury wouldn't allow me to break. Angry tears welled in my eyes. I wiped them away and slipped the tunic over my head to focus on something else for a moment.

Finn, though, was sputtering angrily, trying to articulate a cohesive thought. "Blasted stars, Charlie! Do you even realize what kind of danger you are putting yourselves in? The Aramach already have Oli! Do you imagine that I'm just going to hand you over to them as well? What do you think will happen if they learn you are away from the castle?"

"We are not so incompetent, Finn!" I was nearly shouting. "We made it here in one piece, did we not?"

He spun around just as I finished lacing up my trousers.

"That is barely true! You were both delirious and halfway to hypothermia when you arrived. You are going home. It's just a matter of when."

"The last time I checked, I outrank you. You will not order me around!" I pulled myself to my full height, moving closer to him.

"You've picked a fine time to start asserting your authority. You may be heir to the throne, but you will only make it there if I can keep you safe. You are no good to the realm dead." His finger was inches from my nose.

"You are ridiculous!" I swatted the offending digit away. "We are much safer here with you than we would be at Chridhe where we don't know who to trust. Besides, he's my betrothed, Finn. I cannot simply stand by and do nothing." A few more tears slipped down my cheeks, but I swiped at them quickly, determined to stand my ground. "I am here now, and I refuse to just go home."

We stared at each other for a long while before Isla finally broke the silence.

"Now, children," Isla started, placing a hand on both our shoulders. "It will not matter if we are capable of

71

keeping our presence here a secret if you two keep shouting like that."

Finn and I leveled a look at her.

Then he turned back to me, shaking his head at my clothing. "I guess this is better than what you came in."

My anger dissipated for a moment while he helped us put on our buff coats. Even the supple leather couldn't hide my protruding chest. I reluctantly retrieved my pillow from the floor, positioning it under my tunic and belting the buff coat over it.

I still resembled a portly soldier, but hopefully at least not a feminine one.

Isla and I tied each other's hair back while Finn demonstrated a masculine gait. When he was finally satisfied with our progress, he led us out to the stables.

"Do not move from here until I give you the signal," Finn said, handing us heavy winter cloaks.

The delicious smell of savory meats permeated the air around us once more. Glancing over at my friend, I could see the tempting proposition in her brow.

"We could be quick? Finn would never know we were gone." Isla looked up at me pleadingly.

I took only a moment to debate, before nodding in the direction of the food wagons we had passed on the way to the tavern. The measly bowl of stew hadn't been enough to satiate our hunger.

We found ourselves standing before one of the wagons, watching a merchant handling a few of the delicious smelling meat pies.

"How much?" Isla asked. Even though her hood was pulled low, I could imagine she was drooling under it.

The merchant looked at us, confused, and I realized that she hadn't disguised her voice.

"Welcome, lads," he said uncertainly. "How many ye be needin'?"

Isla hastily asked for four, this time remembering to lower her voice.

We tried again to ask a price, but the man refused to tell us.

"Aren't ye wi' the soldiers?" He nodded toward the direction of the stables. "Dinna fash yerself. I cannae make ye pay."

"Thank you, sir!" Isla stuffed a large bite into her mouth.

I took a small gold coin from my purse and showed it to Isla, raising my eyebrow.

"That should cover it." She nodded.

"Thank you, sir, but I insist." I couldn't imagine taking advantage of the man's generosity. Especially when this seemed to be his livelihood.

His face blanched as he looked down at the coin. *Did we do something wrong?*

"Is this not sufficient?" I asked in my deepest timbre.

"No, no, laddie. 'Tis quite sufficient I'd say." He continued to gape at the single coin as we walked away.

"Wha's the big dheal?" Isla asked around mouthfuls of her food.

"I haven't the slightest idea." I finally took a bite of my own pie and completely melted. I didn't even care that the golden crust was flaking down onto my cloak. "Stars! This is delicious!"

We ambled back to the stables, but not before rough hands grabbed the backs of our necks.

"You two are the absolute worst." My brother urged us forward. "Did you even pay for these? Have either of you ever purchased anything in your lives?"

"Of course we did." I let him hear the offense in my voice. "I gave him a gold—"

"Gold?! You gave him *gold*?" Finn's voice rose on that last syllable. "Perfect, Charlie. I tell you to blend in, and you pay a small fortune for a couple of meat pies."

I didn't understand my brother's aggravation, if it meant that much to the man, I was happy to have overpaid.

"And they were worth every single ounce, my darling." Isla smiled up at Finn over another bite of the controversial pie.

My brother couldn't hide the grin that tugged at the corner of his mouth as he looked back at her.

I had to avert my gaze When Oli had looked at me that way, it usually preceded a request for Finn to keep a lookout while we sneaked into a back corner. I nearly chuckled aloud, remembering the last time that had happened, the day he had proposed.

Oli's lips pulled into his familiar half-grin before he tugged me into an alcove near our rooms at the Castle Alech.

"Get lost, Finn," he said to my brother without breaking eye contact with me.

"Better yet, keep a lookout." I shot him a sideways glance.

Finn opened his mouth and I raised my eyebrow, daring him to argue. How many times had I covered for Isla and him?

"Fine," he grumbled, rounding the corner.

Oli pulled me to him, kissing first the engagement ring he had slipped on my finger earlier that day, then each of my cheeks, then my lips. I smiled, leaning closer. His hands cupped the back of my head as he slowly deepened the kiss.

I lost myself in the feel of his lips against mine, his warm hands trailing down my neck to my back. He stepped back with a soft groan.

"We should go. You know my mother doesn't appreciate being made to wait."

I had almost forgotten we were on our way to tea with her. I bit back a sigh, following him from the alcove where he nearly collided with Logan.

Logan's impassive expression didn't change. He nodded at his brother without breaking stride, nearly rounding the corner before he called back over his shoulder.

"Your tiara is crooked, Highness."

Heat rose to my cheeks. My hand flew up to my crown, which was in fact off-kilter.

"Finn!" Oli snapped. "You were supposed to be keeping lookout."

My brother's head peeked around the corner, followed by a smaller, crimson one.

"Sorry." Isla's face was so apologetic, I couldn't help but smirk.

A large white flake fell onto my cheek, pulling me away from the memory. It had started snowing again, and the heavy wool of my cloak was a welcome relief from the cold, wet air. I snuggled into mine, and noticed my brother looking at us, a gleam flashing in his eyes.

"You both still look too feminine. Wait, I know what you need." He stooped over and picked up some of the dirt on the ground and smashed it roughly into our faces. Well, roughly into mine, at least. Isla got more of a caress, by the looks of things.

His hand lingered on her face a moment before he stepped back to congratulate himself on his work, satisfied with our new disguise. Isla smirked, and I had to admit the dirt changed the overall look of her features. We pulled our hoods down low to complete the disguise while he continued to fling more onto our clothing. Our blue cloaks were close enough to the royal blue of the H'Rian kingsmen that we were already markedly less noticeable.

We mounted our new horses, as our previous steeds needed much more rest than this short reprieve had allowed. Finn instructed us to ride toward the back, as far from Logan's lead as we could.

"We'll be riding much faster than you're used to. I need you to keep up the pace and keep your heads down."

Isla and I exchanged anxious looks as we realized for the umpteenth time on this journey that we had no idea what we were doing.

But that ultimately made no difference to me. Oli was out there somewhere, and I was going after him.

CHAPTER 12

On my best day, with a full night of sleep, this ride would have been a challenge. Never mind the icy gale chilling me to my core or the exhaustion of having the fate of two kingdoms and my own future hanging in the balance. As it was, the breakneck pace Logan set was only made bearable because I knew it would get me to Oli that much faster.

It had been pure luck that we had run into Finn and not Logan or one of the other kingsmen in the square asking subtle questions about Oli's capture. The reports were grim. The Aramach had never been active this side of the Condie River until a couple of weeks ago. The townspeople were terrified after years of hearing horror stories trickling in from the west. This was what Brodie had been trying to tell my father.

They are getting bolder.

But everyone was in agreement; they always came from the west. So west we rode. Isla and I didn't wind up in the very back, as Finn considered that a vulnerable position. Instead, we were two positions from the rear with large hulking men squashed on either side of us and my brother behind.

Some of the kingsmen spat insults in our direction, but for the most part, they ignored us. It was an interesting contrast to the deference with which I was normally treated, but the anonymity wasn't unwelcome. I was able to observe my men, including my brother, in a way that was rarely possible.

One of the green-cloaked soldiers, Graham, played with his dagger every time we slowed the horses. Over and over, he flipped it between his fingers and tossed it into the air, catching it without thought. Another Luanian, Clive, kept up a running commentary, most of it riddled with innuendo.

"Are ye done playing with your dagger there, Graham?" Clive teased the fair-haired fellow as Graham was in the middle of another flourish.

"You jealous, sweetness?" Graham gave him a wink.

Clive opened his mouth to retort, but he was cut off.

"Come now, Clive. No need to be bitter just because no one has played with your little dagger lately." Logan's deep voice sounded almost jovial as he slapped the man on the back.

I held back my laughter and glanced at Isla to see if she was holding back, too. I wasn't disappointed. Her cheeks were puffed up, her lips drawn tight, and she was looking everywhere but at the two jokesters.

"What're ye on about?" Clive asked with fabricated

disgruntlement. "I'm only makin' sure he doesn't poke his eye out."

"Or anyone else's." Finn's eyes widened in mockery.

The men threw their heads back, laughing heartily, and Finn joined in. Logan's shoulders shook as he chuckled along with them. I blushed and looked away from the crude joking. I couldn't help but laugh along, however, grateful my voice was lost in the riot.

Watching my brother and Logan interact with the guard, an unexpected stab of jealousy sprung up within me. The few ladies my age had been more interested in my crown than my companionship. Between that and my rigid, solitary schedule, there was little room for friendship or camaraderie. Even Isla had only been present three weeks a year. The closest I had come to what Finn had with his kingsmen was the letters I exchanged with my friends in Luan, and even then, I knew it wasn't the same.

I couldn't blame them for being cold toward us. Finn had apparently told the men we were foppish laird's sons he was forced to bring along for political reasons. I was surprised Logan had bought that story, but Finn said he was too distracted to bother with us. It made sense.

Growing up, Logan and Oli were inseparable. Oliver was an only child, so when his half-brother showed up after years of being raised in the villages, Oli had been thrilled. It never occurred to him that a bastard son of a king wasn't the most socially acceptable playmate.

He made sure it never occurred to anyone else, either.

This was likely the longest the two had been separated since then.

"Halt!"

Speak of the devil...

I tugged on Isla, and we both ducked a little lower, turning our heads in case he should come this way to inspect things.

Finn snorted.

"Relax. He's just calling a water break for the horses and privy break for the men."

Splendid. Here we go again.

At least we had no trouble dismounting in these outfits, apart from the stiffness that came with the hours we had spent on horseback. Isla and I picked our way across the snow to the nearby copse of trees. We could hear Logan's clipped tones perfectly from our vantage point.

"Prince Finnian, what are those two numpty idiots doing on this mission? I would think finding my brother is a higher priority than accommodating some laird, and don't even attempt to persuade me that either o' them knows how to use those swords."

I hadn't considered that our presence could impede the group, but we hadn't had a choice. How many of the men in this very group were traitors? There may have been someone else who was more qualified to bring the message, but we had no idea who we could trust on either side. We had done what we had to do.

"The lads are a bit green, but they're decent riders. I won't let them slow us down." Finn spoke with a hint of warning, like he knew we could hear them. Then, in a softer voice, "We all want to find Oli."

If Logan responded to that, I didn't hear him.

IT HAD BEEN HOURS SINCE WE'D GOTTEN BACK ON OUR horses. Logan had increased our already-grueling pace after midday, and it had been all I could do to keep up. The muscles in my legs were screaming in protest, and my face had long since gone numb. The lack of sleep and food were finally catching up to me.

It didn't help that our ride had been a silent one by necessity. Isla and I had to avoid speaking, since our impressions of being men were both awkward and suspicious. Without being able to keep ourselves awake with conversation, there was nothing to do but listen to the calming sounds of hoofbeats and the low murmur of men's voices. My eyes felt heavy, and my breathing deepened. Every part of me longed for sleep.

I glanced over to see how Isla was faring just in time to watch her slide precariously from her horse. Before I could even call her name to warn her, my brother rode up next to her, reaching forward with lightning-fast reflexes to gently nudge her aright.

The men on either side of us sniggered at the commotion until a harsh look from their prince silenced them.

"Er... thank you," Isla grunted in her deepest voice.

Finn smirked. "Just keep your seat going forward, Lieutenant."

He may have imparted to us the importance of keeping our identities hidden, but now, the open adoration in his eyes was bound to raise eyebrows. I cleared my throat until he noticed and quickly looked away from her, suddenly very occupied with his reins.

My smile faded. *Have I lost the only person who will ever look at me that way?*

CHAPTER 13

I had never seen anything in my life as inviting as the lights of the towne ahead. Night had fallen hours ago, but we had ridden on. Grateful as I was about the commitment to finding Oli, I was tired to the point of deliriousness and practically numb with cold. I nearly cried with relief when Logan passed on word that we would stop for the night in Tuath Towne. Even the trained kingsmen alongside us mumbled their thanks to the stars, so I knew I wasn't alone.

Finn offered to stable our horses while Isla and I headed inside. I had to resist the urge to loop my arm in hers, conscious of how that would appear to the watching men.

"I can't decide if I need a warm cup of mead, food, or sleep," Isla whispered as she removed her cloak.

"All of those things. Definitely." I followed suit, removing the cloak and enjoying the fire's warmth.

It was a day of firsts, it seemed, as I had never before

set foot in a tavern like this one. Even the last place we stayed was nothing like the bawdy room I stood in now. I looked around at the tables full of boisterous men, and glanced dubiously at Isla.

"How do you think we inquire after beverages?" I asked.

She observed the room for a moment. "Pick seats, and I'll take care of the drinks." She strode purposefully to the long bar.

"Ho ye! Two meads, wench!" she yelled.

Seconds later, Finn appeared at her side, face purple with irritation. I snickered to myself, sinking into an empty chair. Then, Isla smirked and playfully shoved him, and I no longer felt like laughing at all.

It had been so easy, a couple of years ago, to picture our futures as bright and shining beacons of hope. I tried to hold on to that hope now, but it was fading fast in the wake of my exhaustion and the endless wave of hits we both seemed to be taking. I shook my head bitterly. I was starting to seriously doubt that either of us would get our happy ending.

I was so caught up in my melancholy thoughts, I didn't notice Logan's presence until he was standing less than a foot from me. It didn't look like he had seen me, so I turned away from him as nonchalantly as I could. He stood frozen, his towering form visible in the corner of my eye, and I held my breath. He seemed to be looking for someone or something.

Even if my brother hadn't impressed upon us the importance of staying hidden for another day, there was no part of me that felt up to having that confrontation right now, in the middle of this room. I exhaled when he finally moved on, grateful I had managed to avoid that unpleasant encounter.

For now, anyway.

I glanced back over to the bar to see Isla carrying two heaping plates of food and my brother holding two mugs of mead, glaring in my direction. He tilted his head toward the stairs purposefully, and I rolled my eyes before rising to follow them. At least I had avoided one undesirable conversation.

FINN LOOKED AS WRECKED THE NEXT DAY AS I HAD FELT THE day before. He had spent the entire night in and out of sleep on the floor of our room. I hadn't fared much better. Only Isla appeared to be capable of blocking out the intrusive noises of the couple in the room adjacent to ours.

When morning came, Finn had sent breakfast up while he went to question the townespeople. He returned sooner than I would have expected, insisting there was something off about the village and their unwillingness to impart any useful information about the rebels. He rushed our group out even faster than he had the day before.

Whether he was being intuitive or his ill humor was making him paranoid, I didn't mind the early start. I had woken feeling, if not refreshed, at least renewed with a sense of determination to replace the desolation of the night before. I took comfort in the fact that, despite Logan's issues with me, he had unparalleled skill and he loved his brother. He would bring Oli back to me.

We departed before dawn, Logan and Finn both insisting the sooner we left this village, the better. I hadn't noticed anything strange. But then, my travel experience had been largely limited to visiting the keeps nearest the castle and crossing the lake in the summertime to visit Luan.

I managed to hobble out to the stables and onto my horse, though my stiff legs groaned with every movement. I was beginning to grow accustomed to both that pain and the constant bitter wind in my face. At least it wasn't snowing today.

Yet.

It was amazing how quickly my love of the white, fluffy flakes had turned after several hours of trying to blink them out of my eyes. Their icy sting left my nose and cheeks chapped and raw.

The men were in no better spirits. Clive and another kingsman, Ian, had bickered for the last two miles. Logan finally called back to them to silence their argument.

"Sorry, Captain, but he knows I didn't sleep at all last night, and the bastard won't leave me be." Ian shot Clive an angry look while the latter only laughed.

"Now ye bunch of bairns, none of us slept last night." Logan shook his head. "Especially not that couple down the hall."

There was barely a pause before the whole lot of them were laughing.

More jokes ensued, and I looked over to Isla, my face red from both embarrassment and laughter. Her eyebrow quirked in confusion, as she had slept through the night with ease. I'd explain it to her later.

I looked around at the bawdy group once more.

Here are the finest soldiers Lochlann has to offer. My men. I shook my head, a wry grin still on my lips.

CHAPTER 14

We were riding through a grouping of trees much like the last several we had passed through, when Logan's voice came growling back to me.

"Be on your guard, men."

What does he mean by that?

The kingsmen straightened in their saddles, shoulders tense with anticipation. They didn't have to wait long.

The forest seemed to come alive. Black-clad men spilled onto the road from the broad trees on either side of us. A battle cry sounded as the men threw themselves in front of our horses or on top of them, knocking several riders to the ground.

"Rebels," the guard next to me exclaimed.

The Aramach. My blood ran cold.

Logan was a blur of speed at the front of the procession, felling one man after another. The sound of steel hitting bone and slicing skin resonated in my ears. Horses screamed, but it was nothing compared to the wails from the injured and dying men.

Finn positioned his horse in front of mine and Isla's, his sword-arm moving in a flurry of motion to fend off our attackers. My heart raced, and my hands trembled with fear for Isla, my brother, Logan, and my men. *My men.*

The urge to protect them surfaced, but instead, I was huddled down as close to my horse as I could get, useless once again. Why hadn't my array of lessons included some form of self-defense? Distantly, I remembered Logan mocking me for that once, but I had laughed it off as the concerns of a boy who had been raised in the outer villages.

What would a princess ever need with a sword?

Shaking my head at my own ignorance, I moved to unsheathe my borrowed blade. I couldn't right the wrongs of the past, but I could at least try to help now, to fight. Isla shook with terror next to me, eyes wide as the battle raged around us. But the resolve on her features told me she was thinking the same thing.

The rancid scent of blood and death permeated the air around us, and I would not be this melee's next casualty.

My sword stuck in its sheath and I cursed aloud. I looked up in time to see one of the Aramach as he and his horse crashed into ours, nearly knocking me from my steed. My ears were ringing from the sounds of the braying animals and adrenaline coursing through me. Finn moved swiftly in response, parrying blows that came far too close.

With a great sweeping motion, my brother's sword pierced the man's stomach. He removed the blade from the rebel, steel dripping with blood as the corpse fell to the ground.

I stared down at the lifeless body of the man. That was the first time I had ever seen someone die. I fought the nausea creeping inside me and focused on what was next. The jarring movement earlier had helped loosen my sword. Finally wrenching it free, I grasped the hilt in both hands and pointed it away from myself. I had no idea how to use it, but I refused to cower.

Isla had her weapon in her hands as well but was struggling to wield it. The blade was weightier than her smaller frame could manage. Thank the stars for my brother. I had seen him train with Oli from time to time, but I now completely understood why he would be Captain of my guard. His skill was matched only by that of Luan's Captain.

Logan!

I looked around the melee for any signs of that infuriating scarlet topknot. The more I scanned the area, the more I saw of the gruesome battle. One of the rebels lay gasping for air and begging for the H'Rian soldier to show mercy. I looked away just as the kingsman ran him through with his blood-soaked blade.

Bile rose in my throat. *Where is Logan?* My heart raced; I couldn't see him anywhere. My panic was interrupted by another of the rebels falling against my horse. There was a dagger protruding from the back of his neck. I bit back another curse, swinging my sword as if that would protect me from the dying man.

Finn turned, eyes meeting mine before glancing over at Isla. He nodded to himself, seemingly satisfied that we were unharmed. Isla let out a scream. I blanched as one of our own men advanced on Finn from behind, his intent clear.

"Behind you!" I shouted.

Finn brought his horse around quickly, shock plain on his features when he faced the traitor who had the nerve to ride with our kingsmen. To call himself one of them.

The clashing of steel sounded once more, and my heartbeat pounded in my ears. Everything was a blur. Eventually, Finn managed to knock the sword from the attacker's hand. Grabbing hold of his tunic, he threw him from his steed.

As he fell, the rebel produced a dagger and shoved it into my brother's leg, dragging the blade through his flesh before hitting the ground. Finn toppled from his mount. My younger brother's cry of pain chased away any fear I'd been harboring.

The world slowed around me, though my heart beat wild and fast. The traitor scrambled to his feet and found his sword. His back was to me as he stood over my brother, weapon held high.

I didn't hesitate as I spurred my horse toward the man whose name I'd never learnt, hefting my own blade and bringing it down, with all of my might, onto his neck. He froze, stunned, hand reaching for the wound as he slumped down onto the dirt road. Finn limped to his feet and hovered over the traitor, making sure he was dead.

The sword I had found difficult to use moments ago was now dripping with another person's blood. *I killed him.*

Isla had already dismounted from her horse and was at my brother's side, gauging the severity of his wounds. Her face was impassive, not a hint of the emotion I knew she felt inside, but she breathed out slowly, her shoulders relaxing as no serious injury was found.

A weight lifted from my chest. *If I lost Finn, too...* I shuddered and put the thought away.

Deafening silence filled the air. While we had been distracted with Finn, the battle had ended. What had seemed to last an eternity had probably only been mere minutes. Sounds muffled all around me, my chest heaving as my lungs pulled in cold air. The world continued to move at a slower pace as I took in the scene before me.

I looked down at the bloody blade in my hand, my knuckles white from how tightly I gripped its hilt. A shudder wracked my body. I could hardly come to terms with what I had just seen and done. But at least I had saved my brother.

Slain rebels lay all around us, many of them killed by Finn's own hand. How many times had he done this on patrol? Had it become so commonplace for him at only seventeen?

I had to look away from their sightless eyes fixated skyward, their signature black clothes slick with blood. There were more bodies than I would have expected.

Sorrow for the dead warred with the swell of pride I felt for my men. They hadn't faltered, even when we were outnumbered two-to-one.

Logan's warning saved our lives.

I felt panic all over again. He couldn't have fallen. I'd seen him fighting, and there was no way he... The sight of a green and gold cloak soaked in blood stopped me mid-thought. It was covering a twisted and lifeless form by a tree. My heart leapt to my throat.

Not all of our lives, then.

I let out a breath I hadn't realized I'd been holding when Logan's towering form finally appeared.

Thank the stars, he's alive.

As if he had been summoned by my thoughts, Logan turned from where he was assessing a black 'X' tattooed on one of the rebels' necks.

His eyes blazed into mine, molten fury pouring from them like lava. I wanted to believe that he hadn't heard Isla scream, that he didn't recognize me. He was only upset that two untrained sons of a laird had endangered the lives of his men.

But the truth was in his expression. He had figured out we were here.

And he was not happy about it.

CHAPTER 15

I turned to my brother, effectively blocking Logan from my line of sight.

"Laird Campbell is the closest," I offered dubiously.

"True, but he's a right bastard." Finn voiced my concerns aloud. "MacBay isn't much farther, and he's in the right direction."

"Perfect." MacBay was a fair laird, and his son was one of the few courtiers I could stand. Finn winced in pain, using his good leg to catapult himself back on the horse. I sighed in relief when he rode ahead to tell Logan; I was able to hide in the ranks with Isla, further delaying the inevitable confrontation.

The ride to Gadleigh Keep was somber. The men had brought the fallen kingsman to Logan. I hadn't been able to identify him before, but Clive's limp form hanging between Logan's arms would haunt me for the rest of my life. There was no laughter or joking from the man anymore. It was all gone, along with his life. My stomach twisted into knots and I fought to keep from being sick.

I turned my attention to those riding next to me. Finn and the other injured men kept brave faces on, but there was the occasional groan of pain. Several of them rubbed at their eyes each time they looked over at Clive. Isla was silent at my side, barely moving other than to examine my brother every time his face twitched.

I felt numb. Drained. And the surroundings only intensified those emotions.

Passing the Condie River, it was as though someone had turned the page in a picture book. I had heard of the effects of the war from the soldiers and those who came to petition in court, but I was unprepared for the sight of the devastation lining even the main road of H'Ria.

Charred houses no one had bothered to rebuild sat in empty, overgrown fields. An entire village lay in decades-old ruins. Where had its inhabitants gone? Had they all been casualties of war, even this far north? Or, having fled, had they created a new life for themselves some-where, removing the necessity to return?

I told myself it was the latter.

The patch of desolation gradually abated as we neared Laird MacBay's house. Bit by bit, there were signs of growth, of reconstruction, of life, until we finally arrived at an expansive keep. *Gadleigh.*

It was the laird's son Camdyn who came out to greet us. He was tall and broad-shouldered, blond hair topping an infectious smile that he wore even now. Taking in the state of us, he urged his men to lead the injured to the infirmary. We all stared silently as we watched Clive's body being carried away. I struggled to believe only a few hours had passed since I had heard him joking.

It was only the four of us left to face Cam. I turned my head and tried to blend in with the men while he gave my brother and Logan a hearty welcome. Finn kindly requested for us to stay to have our men and horses seen to.

"Of course," Cam responded. "How many rooms will you require?"

"Three," Logan interjected. "Just three, and preferably close together. The lairdlings can share."

"Not a problem, Captain. Let's get you all cleaned up and maybe then we'll have this story." Cam's smile was genuine.

His eyebrow quirked as he attempted to get a better look at Isla and me before urging us to follow him inside.

Logan kept pace with him, not deigning to look back at us.

Perhaps even he wasn't ready for a confrontation so soon after the death of one of his own.

The few remaining rebels had fled, along with the traitorous Luanian kingsman. There was no time to follow them, not when we had so many injured and needing medical attention.

Finn had lost a decent amount of blood, but the wound itself would heal quickly, according to the healer. He was resting now. Isla hovered over him while I sat in a chair in the corner, trying not to focus on the pallor in his cheeks.

A blushing servant girl came to the door with a tray of food for my brother. His body was hard from training and only half-dressed, so I could hardly blame the poor girl. Isla had no such compunctions. She pasted on a smile that was more a baring of her teeth and practically yanked the tray away before the girl could get any closer to Finn. I suppressed the ghost of a smile threatening to appear on my lips.

Though my friend's hands were steady, lines of worry etched her forehead. She had made little effort to appear as anyone but herself once we'd closed the door to Finn's room. If the healer thought her behavior odd, he declined to comment.

I patted Isla on the shoulder, handing her the glass of whiskey I had been nursing. We were both in need of its steadying effects.

A polite knock on the door preceded Camdyn's entry. I turned my head, ready to duck out of the room when his voice interrupted me.

"Princess Charlotte." He said my name nonchalantly, but his grin belied the words. "Would you like to fill me in, or shall I come up with my own explanation as to why the Prince is injured and you're dressed as a man?"

"The latter," I responded drily.

He laughed.

"Very well. Keep your secrets. Let me know if I may be of any assistance."

Camdyn left, but not before sweeping me into an encompassing hug. I broke it off, not wanting the kind gesture to elicit tears.

"Thank you," I called after him. "Truly. For your kindness and your discretion."

He inclined his head respectfully, then shut the door behind him.

With my brother stable and in capable hands, I finally made myself head down the hall to the room I would share with Isla. I could stand a moment to clear my head, but more importantly, I needed to wash off some of the blood and grime coating my body.

Camdyn had generously provided a change of clothes for us, offering to have our bloodstained coats cleaned. There was an urn by the wash basin, covered to keep the water warm.

Stripping down to my thin shift and my brother's underpants, I set the bloodied clothes out in the hall for one of the servants to retrieve. My hands trembled as I removed my necklace, followed by the long strips of cloth that had bound my chest. I filled the basin, then reached for the provided bottle of sandalwood oil. I could hardly keep my grip on it long enough to let a few drops out.

Get it together, Charlie.

I dipped a cloth into the tepid water, then proceeded to wash my hands and face. It felt good to clean myself after three days of travel. Soaking the cloth, I brought it back to my neck. The water soothed every part of my skin it came in contact with, but I still felt numb inside. The warmth couldn't quite allay the disquiet of my soul.

The door to the room jolted open, stopping just short of slamming against the wall. I spun around. Logan's massive frame filled the doorway, eyes burning with fury. He reined in his temper enough to gently ease the latch in place behind him. He hadn't yet changed out of his own tunic, still spattered with blood that wasn't his own.

I let him fume in silence for a moment, not sure what I would say anyway.

"Care to tell me what you're doing here, masquerading as a kingsman and jeopardizing this entire endeavor?" His deep voice came out closer to a growl.

I spun around to place the cloth back in the bowl, taking longer than was strictly necessary, before I turned back to respond.

"I had a message to deliver." I knew it wasn't the explanation he deserved, but it was the only one I had the energy to give.

He squeezed his eyes shut.

"Of course ye did. And you couldn't possibly leave said message to one of the many trained, competent messengers residing in the palace." His voice rose with each word.

My numbness was pushed out by stronger emotions. "I am competent, you condescending arse. I just competently killed someone."

He continued as though I hadn't spoken. "Because then you wouldn't have an excuse to be traipsing around, endangering my men and people you claim to love."

That hurt after my brother's near miss this morning. It was also entirely unfair. I opened my mouth to explain, but once again, he barreled over me.

"Let's no' even concern ourselves with the inconsequential matter of the fate of our two kingdoms. Was it not enough that my brother went missing? You thought you should as well?"

"I left a note." The words sounded feeble, even to my own ears. I took a moment to gather my thoughts and tried to explain myself better. "There was no one at the palace we could trust."

"Why not?" Logan's brow furrowed.

I opened my mouth to answer, but realization washed over his face. He cut me off in a voice that was quieter and so much worse than the yelling a moment ago.

"You knew about the traitors."

It wasn't really a question, and even if it had been, my silence was answer enough.

"Did Finn know?" he asked, eyes narrowing in fury.

I looked away.

"And not one of you thought to tell me before Clive was killed as a result?" His voice wasn't so quiet now.

"We thought you would send us back," I tried to explain. "And we didn't know who to trust."

Something flashed in his eyes, something I might have called hurt on anyone other than Logan. "So, you couldn't trust me, then?"

"That's not what I said." But admittedly, he wasn't wrong. We hadn't trusted his reaction, and we hadn't been willing to risk it.

And now, someone was dead because of our choices.

"No, Highness." The title was cold on his lips. "But it's what you meant."

Silence descended, cold and empty in the air between

us. After a moment, Logan's eyes traveled downward. I followed his gaze to the bare skin we had both been too worked up to notice earlier. Groaning, I crossed my arms over my chest where my shift left little to the imagination. I forced the blush from my cheeks and waited for him to look away.

When another minute passed without a word, I turned back to the wash basin. Finally, I heard retreating footsteps and the click of his hand resting on the door handle. He paused.

"For what it's worth," he said quietly, "as far as the rebel went, you did what you had to do. Just as any of my men would have."

My eyes widened, and tears pricked them. I nodded without turning around. Moments later, the door clicked open and then shut behind me, and finally, I let the tears fall.

CHAPTER 16

My brother was awake by the time I pulled myself together and walked back to his room. A weight lifted off my chest. At least he wouldn't die for the choices we had made these past two days. Isla looked as relieved as I felt, the worry lines gone from her brow.

I hardly had a chance to greet them before Finn's door opened with considerably more care than mine had earlier, and Logan strode in. Though he was furious less than an hour ago, no one would have known it by his placid expression.

"Logan…" My brother sounded like he was about to explain but paused.

"Finn, I'm pleased to see you're doing well." He turned to his cousin. "And, Isla, lovely to see you here. Among my men. Dressed as one of them." His civil expression didn't quite match his tone.

"Ach! Logan. Pull that stick out of your arse, will you?

It's a wretched situation, and we've all done what we felt we had to do." Isla leveled Logan with a challenging gaze.

His face reddened as he opened his mouth to respond, but I held up my hand.

"My brother is recovering in here, *that* is what this room is for," I reminded him. "I'm assuming you came here for something aside from an argument?"

"I did, actually." Logan looked at me, his formal tone never wavering. "I came to tell you that since half of our men are injured and another two were traitors, I've decided it would be better if I continued on alone to retrieve Oliver."

I stilled. If he left to find Oli on his own, we would have no news. They could both be killed, and we would never know.

"No." The word escaped my lips before I had time to consider it. "You can't just make that decision without consulting any of us."

His eyes widened in disbelief. "Oh? The way that you did?" He continued without waiting for a response. "And as the highest-ranking member of my kingdom on this mission, I have every right to make this decision without consulting you, Highness. You may be a princess, but you are not mine."

My mouth dropped open and fury burned my eyes. I wanted to slap his smug face.

Fortunately, Isla responded before I could.

"Brilliant, Logan. We get attacked, Finn gets injured, Clive died, and gallivanting off on your own is the best plan you could manage?"

Sadness washed over the room at the reminder of the kingsman who gave his life in this search for Oli.

"I'm not the one *gallivanting* anywhere. This is my job, cousin. The two of you have done nothing but risk your lives and the lives of others coming out here." Logan's words were quieter, but the anger and disappointment were still evident.

"Peace." My brother was the next to speak. "I know you're worried, Isla, but Logan isn't wrong." He placed his hand on hers while he continued on, ignoring her look of betrayal. "He's the most competent person here, and he's far safer without the kingsmen drawing attention to him."

I didn't miss how he avoided addressing Logan's statement, sure that he agreed with him.

I reluctantly murmured my assent, the days' events still fresh in my mind. If anyone could bring Oli back, it was Logan.

"At least eat something before you go." Isla pointed to the heaping tray of food we had hardly made a dent in.

Logan's face softened at her acceptance. He had never been able to stay mad at his cousin for long. He filled one of the small porcelain plates and sank into a chair between Isla and me.

There was a curious, bittersweet feeling at the four of us sharing the same space again, but the sweet was quickly chased out by the bitter when reality crashing in.

Oli was gone, Logan hated me, and Finn and Isla would never get to be together. When had our lives gone so terribly awry?

I WAS PACING THE FLOORS OF OUR VAST CHAMBER WHEN Isla walked in, suspicion written in the lines of her face.

"You're going with him."

It wasn't a question, but I nodded anyway.

"I really have awoken the beast, haven't I?" Her tone was amused, but her deep green eyes were wide with concern.

"I can't just sit here and do nothing but stew and wait for news, Isla. Besides, the sooner Oli and I are back together in the same place, the sooner we can put to rest any rumors of the treaty being unfulfilled." Images of slain men and abandoned villages filled my head. That would not be my legacy, not if I could help it. "As soon as Logan finds him, we can head to the nearest keep and stop thoughts of war before they have a chance to fester."

Isla's fair skin paled further. "Do you think it will come to that?"

In truth, I had tried not to think about it at all. Luan and H'Ria had years of war between them. I wanted to believe they appreciated the past eighteen years of peace as much as I did, but tensions had never entirely faded.

"I don't know," I answered after a pause. "It's hardly a chance we can take."

Isla's features hardened into resolve. "I'll help you pack."

CHAPTER 17

Dusk was falling when I left to follow Logan. The ruse of being a laird's son from the north had been enough for the guards to allow me to leave without question, if not without judgment. They begrudgingly supplied me with a horse that was more rested. I had simply mounted the mare, tucking my sword into the saddle sheath, and headed out of the keep.

I left shortly after Logan did. If I allowed too much distance between us, I would have to find a way to track him.

Because tracking is clearly among my many skills. It must have been included in the lessons on flawless curtseys or proper riding attire.

I shook my head. Nonetheless, my decision was made. At least the snow allowed me to follow his trail with relative ease. He appeared to be following the main road west.

Pulling the hood of my cloak lower, I followed the path I had seen Logan take.

After riding for about an hour, the sun had set entirely. I could barely make out the hoof-prints in front of me, thanks to the full moon. Not being able to see into the woods around me reminded me of our earlier attack. We hadn't seen any sign of the rebels until the last possible moment, in daylight. How could I imagine faring any better when the darkness would completely conceal their approach?

I shivered, more from the memory than the cold. Finn had barely had time to shield Isla and me before the onslaught began.

I can't believe I killed a man. The abrupt thought echoed through me, making me feel hollower each time it ricocheted in my head. *I killed a man.*

I looked down at my gloved hands as if his blood still coated them, and bile rose in my throat. Logan had said it's what any of his men would have done.

I did what I had to do to protect my brother. I tried to take comfort in that.

It had been the traitor or Finn. I would make the same decision a thousand times over if it meant saving his life, but I never would have imagined that I could be capable of—

What was that?

My horse whinnied and pulled to the left, clearly spooked. A quick glance around revealed nothing but trees and fresh snow.

Fresh snow.

My heart skipped a beat as the world slowed down around me. Where had Logan's tracks gone?

Trying to maintain any semblance of calm, I searched behind me. Only my own horse's hoofprints marred the path. My mount brayed again and pulled strongly to the left. I tried to spur her on, but she continued fighting me, forcing us to stay in the middle of the road. I had never wished more for my fat, compliant mare. Ashwyn would never act like this. The steady warhorse I'd been riding before would also have been preferable.

Hoofbeats sounded just behind me and to the right. I pulled the reins tightly and spurred my mount again. She finally listened and took off at a much faster pace, but I could hear the person behind gaining on us.

Blasted stars! What have I done?

I cursed myself for losing Logan's trail, trying not to let my fear take hold. But several of the Aramach had gotten away. I couldn't help the churning in my gut that told me I had found them again. Or they had found me.

A low grunt and a rustling sound were my only warnings before I was knocked from my horse.

I hit the ground with a thud, and the air whooshed out of my lungs. I watched helplessly as my horse kept running down the dark road until she was completely out of sight. There would be no escape for me.

Between my hood that was covering my face and the crushing weight of my attacker straddling me, I couldn't breathe. My lungs burned, but the icy chill of the dagger at my throat kept me from moving. My eyes began to water.

Breathe, Charlie!

Deep, rasping, painful breaths finally started to fill my lungs, and I coughed violently as air tried to move the other way. The pressure from the rebel's blade lessened and suddenly my hood was ripped away from my face.

"Damn it, blasted woman! What are you—?" Logan's deep voice had never made me happier, nor more afraid. Despite him recognizing me, the blade in his hand was still at my throat, and he made no move to pull it away.

"Logan?" I coughed out. "I—"

"What in the hell are ye doing out here?" There was nothing but unadulterated fury dripping from his every word.

"I... I'm coming with you to get Oli." I didn't have a clever response for him, nor a dignified one. Just the truth.

His responding laugh was cold, disbelieving. There was no joy in the sound.

"Would you care to remove yourself from my person now?" There. That was dignified.

He made no move to comply, only continued to sit atop me, shaking his head at whatever humor or irony he saw in the situation.

"Logan, I'm freezing, and my clothes are soaked through now. Move. Your. Arse." With the bitter chill that was setting in my bones, I didn't find anything at all amusing about the situation. If there was a way to get to Oli that didn't involve Logan's presence, I would have gladly taken it.

Yet, here we are.

He looked down at me, face barely visible in the moonlight. Something flashed in his eyes for just a moment before he finally moved to stand up. I tried to follow suit, but my feet slipped on the icy road. Before I could right myself, Logan roughly grabbed hold of my arms, planting me firmly upright.

I shrugged away from his grip, declining his unwelcome assistance. I moved to brush the residual snow from my back and legs. My cloak had protected most of my clothing, but I was still shivering from the damp weight of the wool against me.

Logan walked back toward his horse before stopping to rub his temples. The tension rolling off him was palpable. Finally, he looked up at me, clearly exasperated.

"So, where are we headed?" I preempted whatever he had been about to say.

"Unless..." I continued on, ignoring the fury written on his features. "Unless you'd like to waste time doubling back? Or perhaps you would prefer me to walk the several miles back to the keep in the middle of the night, unarmed, seeing as you spooked my horse? Of course, I'd just follow you again." I moved toward him and the only mount left.

The redness of his face nearly matched the hue of his hair as he crossed his arms and stared down at me.

"Of course, Highness."

I narrowed my eyes at his acceptance, but he wasn't finished.

"Seeing as you've, once again, managed to manipulate the situation to get your own way. Far be it from me to stop you from inserting your completely inept and unnecessary presence on this mission." He gestured to his horse with false gallantry, his features murderous.

Was that how he saw my coming along when I was only trying to find my fiancé and help my country avoid war? I wondered when Logan had become so determined to think the worst of me. Brushing that aside, I hefted myself onto the horse. Whether I entirely trusted his easy acquiescence, this was the best option to move forward.

Logan's weight settled behind me, angry puffs of breath in my ear. His arms wrapped around either side of me as he grabbed the reins, spurring the horse into a canter. The frigid wind stung my face as we sped off. Between my damp cloak behind me and the blasts of air in front of me, I was chilled to the bone.

Before I knew what he was doing, Logan unclasped my cloak and moved it to his saddle bag. I didn't get a chance to be upset with him about it, because just moments later, he wrapped his own cloak around us both, pulling me in closer to him.

That was unexpectedly... kind.

"Your cloak was getting me wet," he grunted behind me.

Ahh. That makes much more sense.

I couldn't help but think of the last time I was this close to Oli. Another shiver went through me, both from the warmth of Logan compared to the cold I'd been feeling and from the memory of Oliver.

When I had taken off after Logan, I hadn't given much

thought to propriety. *Hadn't given much thought at all*, I reluctantly admitted to myself.

Logan was to be my brother when I married Oli, but that fact wouldn't save us from gossip if we were found with me wrapped in his cloak, arms around my waist to hold the reins.

We wouldn't be discovered, though. We were both dressed in nondescript men's clothing. No one would recognize us. It would be fine.

I hope.

With that thought to calm my nerves, fatigue settled into me like a heavy fur cloak. I tried to stay awake, but my body must have decided there had been enough fighting lately. It wasn't long before the warmth surrounding me and the rhythmic clopping of hooves lulled me under.

CHAPTER 18

His hands wrapped around my waist, pulling me closer to him, the heat of his breath warming each place his mouth lingered. My body arched back into his, not wanting this moment to end but desperate for what I knew would come. Slowly, he unfastened the back of my dress, each button a mountain to be conquered. His fingers, though, were deft, and nothing would stop him from the victory he was owed.

The white velvet finally slipped away from my shoulders, slowly sliding down past my hips and pooling at my feet. I turned to face my husband. Oliver's gaze lingered over my frame, taking in every inch of me. Finally, our eyes met, a gorgeous smile painting his features. I loved that smile.

I had waited and waited for this day to come, and it was finally here. He was mine, and I was his. Oliver leaned in, pressing his lips to my own. Something about this felt wrong, but I pushed the feeling aside. Oli was here. My Oli. His hands slid down my shoulders, and my heartbeat thundered in my ears, so loud, it was almost like... hoofbeats.

I jolted awake. My cheeks were flushed and not from the cold. I felt a little too warm, actually. I was cradled completely against Logan, my head resting in the crook of his neck. I jerked forward, embarrassment flooding through me. I could only pray I hadn't been talking in my sleep.

It felt very... wrong, to have a dream about Oli while enveloped in his brother's arms. I shuddered a little and sat up a bit straighter. The distance did nothing to help the fire coursing through me, so I pulled out of Logan's cloak. Even the chilly air couldn't combat the ever-rising heat of my embarrassment.

Logan was conspicuously silent behind me. I reminded myself that, despite how he managed to make it appear, he was not a mind reader. It was likely that he was only silent because he was still angry with me. I certainly wasn't going to ask him about it.

We were on a stretch of road that looked much like our earlier path. Moonlight glinted off the icy branches of the endless row of trees, and the road seemed to stretch forever. Deep, rolling hills covered in sparkling white peeked from behind the trees. A few houses peppered the hills in the distance, candlelight winking through the windows, and ahead of us were the capped peaks of the Masach Mountains.

They were so much bigger here than our view at the

castle made them seem. If we were this close to them, how long had we been riding?

Only one way to find out.

I voiced the question aloud. There was no response. I tried a different one.

"Do you know where we're stopping for the night?"

Silence greeted me. Frustrated, I whipped my head around to look at him. Logan's stony face was inches from mine, and his features were closed off entirely. If I hadn't known better, I might have believed he actually hadn't heard me. His expression was too controlled for the level of nonchalance he was purporting, however.

"You're stuck with my company for the next several days, at least, Logan. You may as well stop ignoring me now," I needled at him.

His mouth tightened, and I smiled.

Let's see him pretend not to hear me now.

He kept his stare focused straight ahead on the dark road yawning before us. Being this close to him, I could see the small lines creasing the corners of his eyes. Once I noticed that, other signs of exhaustion became evident. The dark circles under his eyes contrasted with the redness that lined them. The deep grooves along his forehead and between his furrowed brow gave away how worried he was, as well.

There was something else there on his features that I couldn't quite put my finger on. Sadness?

I'd been lost in my silent observations for a time before realizing that he was staring back at me. Once our eyes met, he stiffened and shook his head briefly before looking straight ahead once more.

"Why are you ignoring me? Is this about today? Or is this about Oli? Are you being a bigger arse than usual because you're worried?" I had to dig deep to dredge up sympathy for him in the wake of his constant brooding rudeness.

He had the nerve to chuckle. Whether it was from humor or irritation, though, I couldn't tell.

"We've lost too much time, so we may not find a place that accommodates your standards, Highness."

"What…?" I trailed off as I remembered the first question I had asked him. Of course, that would be the only one he would answer.

"I think you'll find that my standards aren't quite as high as you assume, Logan."

He arched an eyebrow. "Yes, Highness."

I turned back around, having no further desire to see his contrary smirk.

"Where are we headed? Can't you at least tell me that?"

"Bala."

I considered what I knew of the area around the Bala Dam. It was known to be loyal, but Brodie had brought strange reports of the area, sightings of the Aramach and disturbances in the villages surrounding it. His men should be there now, in fact. Why would we go also?

"Why?" I voiced the question aloud.

I received only a sigh in response. It was going to be a long ride.

CHAPTER 19

We rode in silence for another few hours before Logan's arms slackened around my waist, the exhaustion catching up to him. He couldn't continue like that without proper rest. Neither could I, for that matter.

Village lights sparkled in the distance. Perfect. We could take a rest and maybe even purchase another horse, so I wouldn't have to ride with the surly man anymore.

Perhaps that will make this journey a bit more tolerable.

With a sigh, I took control of the reins with one hand and held onto both of Logan's with the other. After anchoring him to me, I prodded the horse into a canter.

The sooner we reached this village, the better. Logan's hands stirred under my own but then relaxed again as he drifted back to sleep. He didn't wake up until we came to a stop in front of an inn.

"Woah, easy boy." The poor beast was probably as tired as we were.

"What?" Logan began to ask.

"This seems as good a place as any to stop for a rest," I offered, dismounting. The biting air crept in where his body heat had been, and I fought down a shiver.

Logan bristled. "Do you realize how much ground we've yet to cover?" His high-handed tone grated at the last vestiges of my nerves. Things had been so much more peaceful when the steed and I had been the only ones awake.

I knocked on the solid wooden door before responding. "Yes, I'm certain we would have gotten a great deal accomplished, not to mention been ready to defend ourselves, what with you asleep on the horse."

Just then, the door opened. I turned toward the inn, using what remained of my good will to steer myself away from stomping on Logan's unsuspecting foot.

Logan fumed behind me but said nothing. The stout, frizzy-headed woman standing before us was too busy staring at Logan, now bathed in the moonlight from the doorway, to notice the oddity beside him. I looked him over objectively: broad shoulders gave way to a body hardened by training, topped by jade eyes and scarlet locks. I supposed I couldn't blame her, given that she wasn't subject to his personality.

"Ye'll be needin' lodging then?"

"One room, please." His deep voice held none of the disdain he was constantly directing at me.

The innkeeper was leading us both indoors, naming a price, when my foggy brain decided to process what he had said.

"Two," I corrected. I was far enough in the shadows, and the woman had been clearly roused from sleep. I hoped she wouldn't look too closely at me.

Logan's shoulders tensed, but he didn't turn. "One will be fine," he assured the woman, who had still hardly glanced in my direction.

I started to speak again, but his words trod over mine.

"Ye can never be too careful." Though he kept his tone light, the comment was pointed.

The innkeeper shook her head, her curls wobbling precariously from their pins with the motion. "Naw, laddie. That ye canne. Will ye be needin' anything else?"

"Just a stable, please," Logan answered.

Two pleases in one conversation? I hadn't even been aware he knew that word. Even road-weary and irritated, I knew that thought was unfair. There had been a time Logan had used the word freely. Even in the wake of his mother's death, adjusting to the political climate and a family he had never known, Logan had been unfailingly polite to everyone.

Of course, thinking of a younger Logan inevitably brought me to Oli. Somehow, I doubted the Aramach were as susceptible to his charm as the palace cooks had been. A pang went through me, memories flooding my mind.

A younger, but no less handsome Oli, talking our way out of trouble after we had played hide-n-seek in the kitchen and nearly upended the king's evening meal. Oli, holding his hand out to me tentatively, for the first time, and how warm it had been when he closed it around my own. Those same sure fingers slipping his grandmother's ring onto my third finger, promising his life to me. The betrothal had been in effect since our birth, but that declaration was his alone.

I was pulled from my reverie by a rough hand on my arm.

"Time to go up." Logan was already moving toward the stairs.

I followed, my bleary eyes barely taking in the sight of the sooty stable boy stumbling out to care for the mount. My legs trembled up two flights of steps, but I managed to keep pace with Logan until we entered our single room. With a single bed. There was a screen to the left I could only assume concealed a washing tub, and very little else in the cramped space.

I stood uncertainly in the doorway. Logan walked over to the bed and moved his hands to untie his sword belt. I looked away, cheeks reddening. This was ridiculous. I was supposed to have been a married woman, and it's not as though he was removing any actual clothing. Still, I kept my eyes safely averted while he bent down to also take his boots off.

Just as I opened my mouth to ask where he intended to sleep, he plopped unceremoniously onto the bed, eyes already closed.

"Logan," I muttered.

He groaned. "Where'd you expect me to sleep?"

"In another room. Like I suggested."

"There are rebels about. Just go to sleep, woman. It's

not like I'm going to touch you." He said that last part with his usual disdain.

My eyes narrowed. I deliberated for a moment. True, we had been close on the horse, but I had never shared a bed with anyone aside from Isla, and she didn't count. I had imagined that would be one of many firsts with Oliver, and this felt like a betrayal. Logan's snores interrupted my inner turmoil. Clearly, he wasn't taking this half as seriously as I was.

"Fine. I suppose you're happy to shoulder the risk of being caught sharing a bed with the princess. I do hope you aren't too attached to that giant head of yours," I hissed, aggravated by his sleeping.

He stirred. "I don't see any princesses in this room, do you?"

I looked down at my travel-stained men's clothing and could not disagree. With a groan, I dragged myself to the other side of the bed and removed my boots. Frigid air hit my toes, and I hurried to blow out the lamp before I burrowed into the covers. Or tried to, but Logan's bulky form weighed them down to his side of the bed. I tugged twice to no avail.

"Get off the blanket!" I hit his arm with slightly more force than was strictly necessary.

He heaved a sigh before obliging me. That was better. Now only my feet were cold. At home, the servants would bring warm bricks for the bottom of my bed, but I doubted the inn offered any such luxury.

I tossed and turned, unable to relax enough to find a comfortable position. Each time I did, my mind raced from one anxious thought to the next. *How is Finn? Is he healing? Are he and Isla heading back to the castle yet?* I had no doubt Isla would be safe if she stayed with my brother.

I snorted a laugh as I thought about the reverse being true as well. Finn would be safe from the attentions of the servant girls, at least. My friend would make sure of that. My smile died as I considered where my fiancé might be. I said a silent prayer for his safety, not allowing myself to consider the danger he was in.

My stomach churned, and I shivered, my blood running even colder. I grunted as I flipped in the bed once more. I was so exhausted but couldn't shut my mind off from the thoughts assaulting me.

The minutes continued to tick by, and my feet refused to thaw. My wool socks weren't helping at all. I couldn't sleep with my toes half frozen. I kicked the blankets, irritated at myself, my cold feet, and my anxious mind.

"Damn it, woman! Why are ye not sleepin'?" Logan barked the question, clearly annoyed.

"I can't!" My frustration was just as evident as his.

I slipped my socks off, attempting to warm my feet with my hands, but it was useless.

After only a small deliberation, and without any thought whatsoever to his disgusted tone when he said he wouldn't touch me, I moved my legs across the bed to place my freezing toes against Logan's calf. I wiggled them until I found a spot between his sock and his trousers. I enjoyed a split second of relief before he yelped and moved his calf away.

"Ach, woman! Don't do that."

I got a perverse pleasure from inflicting some of my own dissatisfaction back on him.

"Do this, you mean?" I said, putting my foot back on his bare skin.

He pulled his leg away again, grunting irritably.

I shuffled my feet furiously, fully aware how childish it seemed. "If you'll just let me get my feet warm, we can both sleep."

Logan grumbled, but finally moved his leg slowly back toward me, which I took as his tacit consent. A satisfied sigh escaped me as the warmth seeped back into my feet. I snuggled further into the blankets with only my eyes exposed to the cool night air.

Looking over at Logan's still form, I couldn't help but think how different he looked from his brother.

It should be Oli lying next to me.

Sadness crept in at the notion. I couldn't help but wonder if I would ever get the chance to lie this close to him. The night before we were to be married, I'd had that opportunity.

Part of me wished I had never left his room. If I'd stayed, maybe I'd be sleeping next to him, wherever he was, instead of here next to his cantankerous brother. Although the idea of being with Oli was preferable to my current company, the thought of both of us in the hands of the rebels was terrifying.

Despite my sullen thoughts, somewhere between my finally-thawing toes and the even sound of Logan's breathing, I managed to drift off into a dreamless sleep.

CHAPTER 20

The few hours of deep sleep had been exactly what I'd needed. For the first time in days, I felt rested and peaceful watching the dust dance in the rays of sunshine filtering in through the small window. I rolled over to see if Logan was still asleep, but the bed was empty.

Logan was gone.

I leapt up, looking around the small space as if that would change the fact that he wasn't in it. My breath caught in my throat.

No. That bastard didn't leave me. He wouldn't dare.

My heart pounded as I ran through my options for what I would have to do next. If I bought a horse, I could still catch him. I knew he was headed to Bala. I was pulling my boots on when a knock sounded at the door. I hobbled to answer it, one boot on my foot and the other in my hand.

"Guid Mornin'... Miss?" The small stable boy from last night stood before me, obviously confused about my sex.

Glancing down, I could see why. My long hair had come out of its knot, cascading over the tunic I had paired with men's trousers.

"Yes, lad. What can I do for you?"

The child smiled and entered the room with a small tray filled with breakfast meats, breads, and tea. The smell of bacon almost chased away all my previous concerns. Almost.

"What is all this?"

"The sir tell'd me tae give this to ye." He set the tray down on the bed, then pulled a note from his pocket. It was from Logan.

Stay in the room. Don't do anything reckless. Be back later.

I let out an unladylike snort.

Like hell, I'll stay here.

"Would ye like me tae draw ye a hot bath, miss?"

I stilled, taking stock of the grime still coating my body from yesterday's skirmish and another day on the road. My aching muscles didn't help matters.

Staying here would be the responsible thing to do.

ORDINARILY, SOAKING IN A HOT BATH WOULD HAVE BEEN A comfort, but all I could think of was Oli. While I was safely enjoying these small luxuries, he was a prisoner. I had no idea if he was hurt or even alive at this point. I cleared my throat as if that would hold back the tears threatening to fall.

This was the first time I had truly been alone with my thoughts. Every moment since Oliver was taken had been rushed and panicked, but sitting here in the warm water forced a clarity to my mind.

I replayed each action I had taken that had led up to the bath and shook my head at some of my decisions. At the time, each one had seemed perfectly rational. In hindsight, I had clearly been telling myself whatever I needed to in order to get to Oliver. I couldn't honestly regret my actions. Besides, I would have quite a story to tell him once we were back together.

If we are ever back together.

I couldn't think that way now. I had to believe we would find him. I wouldn't give up hope. My stomach threatened to revolt against the breakfast it had devoured only moments ago. I set the last bite of my bacon back down on the tray and looked away from it, breathing deeply in an effort to gain control over my precarious gut.

I stood to step out of the bath just as the door suddenly banged open. I froze, grateful for the screen shielding me from view. It was apparently doing its job a little too well, though. Logan cursed.

"Blasted woman. I told her to stay put."

I narrowed my eyes, though he couldn't see me. "The blasted woman did stay put, and requires a towel at your convenience."

There was a lengthy pause before something came sailing over the screen. I caught it before it hit the water.

"Thanks ever so much." I wrapped the small cloth around myself and tried not to shiver. My hair was piled on my head and still mostly dry. I opened my mouth to ask for my clothes when a bundle of fabric was delivered in the same manner as the towel. I bit back a sharp response.

"These aren't mine," I told him, though that should have been obvious. My filthy trousers bore no resemblance to the rustic woolen dress I was holding.

"We don't have time for your whining, Highness. Just put it on and let's be on our way."

Anger chased away the little bit of relaxation the bath had lent me. I had only been stating the obvious, but he had been damned and determined for years to think the very worst of me.

"There was a time when you were kind, Logan." Last night's memories simmered at the forefront of my mind.

There was a beat of silence, and I wondered if he had even heard me. Then, his voice came clearly through the screen.

"And there was a time when you aspired to more than mediocrity. So, I suppose we've both changed."

What does that even mean? I was going to be queen. I did everything that was required of me. I spent every day preparing for my future role. I hadn't changed at all. What more did he want from me? I opened my mouth to tell him that, but the door slammed shut again.

Fuming, and having nowhere to vent my anger, I dressed with gusto, firmly pulling the dress over my head and shoving my arms through the sleeves. I wasn't sure why he had purchased the gown to begin with.

Shouldn't I still be disguised?

I couldn't deny that the familiarity of the skirts about my ankles was a comfort, though. My tunic and trousers had been an interesting experiment, but I felt more like myself, even in the rustic warm dress. It fit surprisingly well, considering I was a couple inches above average height and a bit, well, bustier.

I left my hair to hang loosely down my back, not wanting to risk styling it in any way that could cause recognition. There was no telling how many of the villagers were among those who came to petition us at open court every week.

A quick glance in the mirror told me I had little to worry about. The simple dress was dyed-green wool with long sleeves and skirts divided for riding. Coupled with my unadorned hair and face, it was disguise enough. Not to mention that no one expected the princess to be roaming around without her guard.

I clutched my ring between my fingers, admiring the beautiful stones on the delicate gold band. Whispering a silent prayer that the giver of this ring was still alive, I gently tucked the chain into the front of my dress, hiding it from view.

Finally throwing on my cloak, I headed out toward the stables. I was determined to confront Logan about our conversation, as well as find out why I needed the wardrobe change. But the sight of him with only one horse stopped me short.

"Where is mine?" Certainly, he didn't expect us to ride together after the way he had treated me.

He stared, wide eyed, at my unbound hair for a prolonged moment.

"What? You wanted me to look like a commoner. Now I do." I looked away, feeling oddly self-conscious.

Shaking his head, he continued without addressing my statement. "Look around, Milady." The title was mocking on his lips. "This is a hamlet. There are no horses for sale. No' everything is about your comfort."

Shutting my eyes, I took a deep breath. I was going to kill him. I was actually going to kill him. Before he could insult me further, I put a foot into the stirrups and gripped the saddle to pull myself up. Logan made a small movement as if to help me, and I made sure my free foot caught him lightly in the chin before swinging it the rest of the way over the horse.

"Real mature." He quietly cursed me under his breath before climbing up behind.

I couldn't help my small smile as he grabbed hold of the reins and encouraged the horse forward.

Riding this way in a dress, even one with divided skirts, was far more difficult than it had been in trousers. But sitting side saddle for the kind of riding we would need to do today was impractical. It also would have forced me to press up against Logan even more than I already had to. Adjusting my skirts brought my earlier question to mind about why I was back in a dress.

"Why did I need to change from my other clothes?" I

asked over my shoulder, sure that he would ignore my query.

Shockingly enough, he actually answered me after a short pause. "Because your disguise was terrible." He grabbed the reins before elaborating. "Ye look nothing like a man, and it will be easier to pretend we are husband and wife if we're to continue sharing a horse and a room. Before you argue, think about the fact that it's the most practical option, and that I'm just as unhappy about it as you are."

It was insulting that he either thought I couldn't see reason or that I would be too emotional to do what needed to be done. Not for the first time, I wondered when I had given him cause to think so little of me.

"All right," was all the response I gave.

Logan stiffened behind me, obviously waiting to see if I would say more. "That's it?"

"Listen, Logan. Just because you find me revolting and I find you obnoxious doesn't mean I'm unintelligent and can't see reason. It makes sense. I wasn't trying to argue. I just wanted to know."

His fists gripped the reins tighter, the whites of his knuckles going taut against the skin. I braced myself, prepared for his temper once more. But it didn't come.

"I never said you were unintelligent." That was all he offered.

It didn't escape my notice that he hadn't argued about finding me revolting. Logan spurred our horse into a gallop, effectively ending the conversation.

There was little sign of life past the village, only miles

and miles of abandoned houses and charred ruins of villages never rebuilt from the war. With mine and Logan's self-imposed silence, I was left with nothing but my own bleak thoughts and the even drearier landscape to keep me company.

CHAPTER 21

"**I**s that smoke?" My refusal to break the several-hours-long silence between us crumbled in the face of my concern.

Logan, of course, declined to respond. I turned to face him with a sigh, ready to throw his accusation of immaturity back in his face. But his features weren't cold or distant as I had expected them to be. They were slack with dread as he stared at the black plumes rising from behind a distant hill.

A hill that was directly in front of Bala.

I turned back in the saddle, and we both spurred the horse to ride faster. The cloying smoke mingled with a pungent aroma reminiscent of the meats roasted over the spit on festival days. My stomach churned, and Logan's arms tightened around my waist. By the time we topped the hill, my heart was already in my throat.

Nothing could have prepared me for the sight that lay ahead.

"Don't look." Logan was trying to turn my body, but I shoved him away and dismounted. These were my people, and I would not look away from what had been done to them.

The bodies were burned beyond recognition.

Snow and ashes mingled in the wind, settling on my cloak and in my eyelashes. I blinked them away, wondering if I would ever again find beauty in the tiny crystalline flakes.

Armor lay strewn across a blood-soaked field, but there were far too many on the pyre to be only the soldiers my father had sent the day before my wedding. These people were innocent. Protruding from the burning mass was a familiar red flag with a black 'X' on it, waving proudly over the carnage its followers had wrought.

The Aramach.

My blood boiled with rage, but I stepped closer. Those on the outside were more intact, singed skirts resolutely refusing to burn. Had their wearers been as stubborn? It had mattered little in the end, I supposed. They had slaughtered the women as quickly as the men.

What kind of monsters are they? And they had Oli.

Logan's footsteps sounded softly behind me. I still hadn't looked away from the pyre.

"Something is wrong." My mind was snagging on a detail, but it wasn't quite processing.

"This entire thing is wrong, Charlie." He said my name softly.

He was right, but that wasn't what I meant. Finally, it hit me.

"Where are the children?" I looked back at him. "Logan, where are they?"

He turned back to the bodies, studying them as I just had.

"Stay here a moment." He waited for my muttered agreement, then headed into the village.

I stared after him, trying to force air into my reluctant lungs. The rebels had already proven they were without souls, without consciences. I had asked where the children were, but I wasn't sure I actually wanted to know.

Breathe, Charlie. But the smoke was assaulting my nostrils; the scent I now recognized for what it was overtook every one of my senses. I fought to keep my breakfast down, but my knees gave out at the same time my resolve did.

I barely registered the sound of Logan's footsteps before I felt his hands brush against my neck, sweeping my hair away from my face. I stayed hunched on the ground, emptying the contents of my stomach until there was nothing left but bile. At long last, the heaving calmed.

I sat up, running my hand through my hair and incidentally dislodging Logan's. He leaned back on his haunches, catching my gaze, and I steeled myself for whatever he was about to tell me.

"They aren't here." His voice was even, and he didn't appear to be lying to spare me.

"There were no children anywhere?"

"No. And somethin' else… the dam has been destroyed."

"That isn't possible." But it was. I realized the sounds of the rushing river had been in my ears, not the stillness I would have expected from the dam. "The Aramach did that?" I continued as though I hadn't just contradicted him.

"We can only assume." Logan's gaze hadn't wavered, like he was trying to anchor me.

"If that was their purpose, then why…" I couldn't get the words out. My throat closed, and I looked away.

"I don't know. To make a point? Bala is known to be loyal to the crown." His words felt far away. The theory made sense, but it wasn't quite registering.

It had been cold when we got here, but now it was freezing, even in the warmth of the gruesome fire. Shivers wracked my body. There was a keening sound in my ears. I shook my head to dislodge it, but Logan leapt to his feet, eyes alert.

I stumbled up next to him, searching for the source of the sound. Had someone survived? The thought propelled me, and I was running before I could consciously register the motion.

"Wait." Logan's hand wrapped around my arm, slowing me. "Just… let me go first."

I stared at him, only barely registering his request.

"Please," he tacked on.

I nodded, and he stepped in front of me, toward the sound. We topped the low hill to find a man dressed in the simple clothing of the villagers, lying in a pool of blood. I barely restrained myself from bounding over to check his wounds, but Logan held his hand out to stop me.

As we approached, a pecking crow flew away with a flutter of wings and an angry caw at interrupting his meal. Nausea seized my stomach. The man had not even registered the beast biting at his ankle.

I took a closer look at the older man. His eyes were closed, and he wheezed uncontrollably. He hardly looked dangerous. I told Logan as much.

Logan knelt next to the man and hooked a finger around his collar, pulling it wide for me to see the black 'X' inked clearly into his skin. My blood ran cold. This man, the only one left alive — though barely, by the looks of it — was one of those who had committed this horrific crime.

My hand went automatically to my waist, but the sword belt had been left behind with the horse.

Damn it!

I reached for Logan's sword, but he blocked me.

"What are you doing? He killed them!" Furious tears burned at my eyes.

"And he's nearly dead himself. He also might have information we need." Logan's tone was too reasonable for my state of mind, but he was right.

I huffed out a breath, gesturing for him to get on with the questioning. He shot me a sideways glance too scrutinizing for my liking before he obliged.

He shook the man gently. "Where we be headed now, sir?" Logan's exaggerated accent was intentional.

The rebel's eyes widened for a moment before the wheezing took on a gurgling sound.

"'Tis alright, 'tis only me."

He looked toward Logan, finally registering our presence, and a smile overtook his bloodied mouth.

"Oh — oye, lad." The man attempted to speak, but his voice was rough and strained. Logan furnished his flask of water and gently helped the old rebel to drink.

I looked away. I was shaking with the horror of what the man had done, but it was still hard to watch another human being suffer the way this man was.

After taking his flask away, Logan repeated his question.

"Where we be headed now?"

I hoped this would work. Wherever their group was headed, they should have the children. The man's eyes widened again, taking in the sight of us, as if he had forgotten our presence. He took a deep, crackling breath and exhaled out, coughing up more blood.

"Needs tae be... Hagail. Prince is..." His slurred words were interrupted by another round of convulsing.

Prince? My prince?

My fingernails gripped Logan's shoulder as I thought about his words. Logan's eyes widened at what the man might mean, and he continued asking questions. Somehow, we would piece this all together.

"What prince?" Logan's voice was soft as he leaned in closer to hear everything the man would tell him.

"Blas-ted Lu-an Prince, o' course. Be takin' him... get

him. 'Agail. H-agail." Logan looked back at me as another fit overtook the rebel.

"What is he saying?"

"I think they have Oli at Hagail." Logan's features were severe, his brows furrowed and his lips drawn in a thin line.

"We have to go after them! Maybe we can still catch them."

The answering stare I received told me more than his words did. There was no way we could catch up with the rebels that had been here.

"Most o' the blood on this man is old. He's been here for at least a day. The rebels won't be anywhere near us now." I had expected him to argue that we would need reinforcements, but his obvious concern was for how far behind we were.

"What do you want to do?" he asked.

It didn't escape my notice that Logan was asking my opinion, which was rare enough to make me suspicious. Then again, this was my kingdom. I deliberated for a moment. We could go back for reinforcements, but we would risk losing our first real lead on Oli.

And what about the children? We were already a day behind them, and any clues to their whereabouts. If we turned back now, we could lose close to a week. True, we couldn't take on the Aramach ourselves, but we could at least find them before they disappeared. There was only one real option.

"We need to get word to my father." I closed my eyes, mentally picturing the map I had studied for as long as I could remember. "The closest village is at the outskirts of the Dorcha Forest. It should be right on the way to Hagail. Then we carry on to find Oli and any sign of the children." I mounted the horse in front of Logan.

His warmth behind me was nearly as familiar as the weight of the cloak. I leaned into him, willing my shivers to still, and for once, he didn't pull away. I supposed, as much as he generally despised me, even he couldn't deny me the small relief of being warm after what we had just been forced to witness.

He dug his heels into the horse's side with more urgency than usual. It seemed I wasn't the only one who couldn't leave that place fast enough.

CHAPTER 22

The wind picked up on our ride, whipping tendrils of hair violently into my face. I tried to close my eyes against the assault, but each time I did, the pyre at Bala was there waiting for me. My eyes stung from more than just the icy gales.

The magnitude of everything that had happened over the last few days was fully catching up to me. I couldn't help but think of Oli, or how only yesterday I was forced to take a man's life. My mind replayed what the Aramach had done to the villagers and what all of those missing children could be going through.

Heaving sobs wracked my body as I mourned each of them in turn. It took some time to regain control of my emotions. Silent tears streamed unbidden down my face.

"I think last time I was in a windstorm like this was that time we were all on the lake. What was it, four years ago?" Logan's tone was conversational, like he hadn't just witnessed me breaking down. "It was Oli's idea, of course. 'Just a little breeze,' he insisted."

I wiped at a tear dripping down my chin and chuckled at the memory.

"We were at least a mile from shore when the worst of it hit. The boat was rocking. Isla was glarin' daggers at Oli…"

"And Finn was a disaster…" My voice was still trembling.

"That he was." Logan chuckled. "He's come a long way."

I thought about Finn's expression when he saw Isla and me at that first village and wondered at that statement. I knew Isla and I were the glaring exceptions to my brother's usual cool-headed nature, though, so I didn't argue. I missed my brother almost as much as I missed Oli. Instead of dwelling on that, I begrudgingly accepted the distraction Logan was offering.

"I seem to recall someone falling in the lake," I croaked out.

"Fallin' is one word for it. Being pushed would be more accurate." Logan's chuckle rumbled against my back.

A ghost of a smile pulled at my lips. "In fairness, you were laughing at Isla and me both."

"It was hard not to when the two o' you were flapping around like a pair of angry hens tryin' to keep your skirts in place."

A laugh bubbled from my lips, and I put my hand over my mouth. The tears threatened to reappear. Laughing after what we had just borne witness to felt like a betrayal of my people, of Oliver.

Logan paused before he spoke again, his tone more serious. "The first time I was sent to subdue the Aramach was during my training to be Captain. It was a massacre. After we left, the captain took the men to a tavern, and I couldn't understand how they could all be laughin'. What kind o' monsters could even smile after what we had seen?

"The Captain must have noticed my expression. He pulled me aside, and I'll never forget what he told me. 'Son, there will always be horrors in this world. You aren't doing those who have died any favors by refusing to live.'"

"Son?" That was the only part of his story I could bring myself to address.

Logan's sigh ruffled my hair. The wind had died down sometime during our conversation.

"Right. You remember what it was like when I first came to court. The Captain took me under his wing."

I did remember. Queen Siobhan was very nearly perfect in appearance, and she knew it. That her husband would stray with a common village woman had been insult enough. When the result of that indiscretion had been thrown in her face at court, the gorgeous woman had been livid. She had done her utmost to ensure Logan wasn't taken kindly to, especially in the beginning.

"That was good of him." I smiled at the warmness of the memory. Speaking of kindness had me remembering our conversation the day before, and my raw emotions made me bold. "Why are you bothering to be nice to me now, Logan? Just because you think I'm suddenly too broken to handle the full force of your winning personality?" I meant for the comment to come out teasing, but it fell flat.

Logan went taut behind me. "I just know a thing or two about talking soldiers down after a battle."

Soldier. I supposed the term fit, what with killing a man yesterday and viewing the slaughter today. Still, it didn't quite sit right with me. I wondered at the changes a handful of days on the road had wrought. *What sort of a queen will I be by the time we return? More importantly, what sort of person?*

CHAPTER 23

"Anything else you care to add?" I asked Logan before I signed the letter.

He scanned it, then shook his head.

"No, I think you've covered it adequately."

I had been so concerned about Oliver, so sure we would find him by now, that the realities of war had felt vague and removed. The selfish part of me longed for that naïveté, but the queen in me would hold fast to the heart-breaking images at Bala. I would do whatever it took to prevent war from visiting our borders again.

I signed the letter to my father and handed it to the messenger along with a sizable stack of coins.

"The king must get this at once," I urged the lithe man.

He looked scarcely older than I was, but he nodded gravely. Now, we only had to hope he was loyal. Would I have questioned such a thing before seeing the reach of the Aramach? Brodie's words from a few days ago came back to me, along with my father's reaction. I had always thought him a good king, but his oversight here made me question that surety.

We ate a quick dinner of stew and bread in the main tavern, but even the substantial noise failed to drown out the thoughts bouncing around my skull with abandon. My eyes caught on my deep green sleeve, and I asked the most innocuous of the questions on the tip of my tongue.

"Where did you find a dress to fit me, anyway?"

Logan swallowed his food before answering without looking at me. "The village seamstress took care of it."

That wasn't an answer, but it was likely as much of one as I would get. Attempting conversation with Logan took more energy than I had left, so we finished our meal in silence. Apparently, he had tapped that well dry earlier.

He had insisted on us sharing a room again for safety. I could hardly argue after what we had just seen, but I was not looking forward to the prospect of another awkward night in the same bed. It was bad enough when he insisted on standing guard outside the privy. I sighed, realizing without the comfortable tunic and trousers of last night, I would be stuck sleeping in this dress.

Logan waited for me to swallow my last sip of ale before inclining his head toward the stairs. I trudged after him to another tiny room on the third floor. The Winter Festival Day was coming up soon, and it showed in the busier taverns and inns.

I didn't bother with lingering in the doorway this time. Instead, I went around to the far side of the bed, stripped off my boots, and climbed in without so much as a look at

Logan. He followed suit, his sword belt clattering against the floor.

It was too quiet up here on the third floor. I could hear Logan's unsteady breathing that told me he was not yet sleeping. I couldn't blame him, not after what we had seen today. Also, it was freezing in the room. *Did people live this way? Were they cold all the time while I was bundled up with my heated bricks in my castle?*

I moved around, trying to nestle my feet somewhere under the yards of fabric in my skirt. I kept my eyes open, avoiding the unwanted image of the pyre at Bala. My hair still smelled of burning things, assaulting my nostrils and making it impossible to leave the memories behind. I took in a shaky breath, shivers and memories assaulting me with equal force.

"You'll be no good to anyone without sleep, woman." Logan's voice was rough with exhaustion.

"I could say the same," I called over my shoulder.

"Ach. I'm a soldier. I'm accustomed to it."

Not for the first time, I wondered at the realities of Logan's life considering he kept a cool head in the face of countless dead villagers and didn't seem to need sleep to function.

I rolled over to look at the hardened man lying next to me. His eyes remained closed while I studied his stony features. Was the kind boy that I had known as a child still in there, somewhere, despite the horrors he'd seen? A weight settled on my chest as I reflected on how differently things had been back then. *How different we had been.*

"Well, I'm a Warrior Queen, so, I'll manage." My voice

came out shaky with the cold. I wasn't sure why I had brought that up, except to avoid talking about anything more serious. Talking about memories wasn't necessarily better. Not with Logan.

My declaration was met with a soft snort. Then, I felt his calf inching hesitantly toward mine.

"Warm your feet up before you break your teeth with all that chattering, oh mighty Warrior Queen."

I debated refusing his offer just to be contrary, but in the end, my pride wasn't worth my icy toes. I pressed them against his calf with a sigh, letting the tiny bubble of warmth chase out every intrusive thought in my head until I finally fell asleep.

CHAPTER 24

W e were on the road before the sun finished rising. Logan had woken me as soon as he had the horse saddled at the barest hint of dawn, but I wasn't complaining. I couldn't bear to think of Oli or the children in the hands of those monsters any longer. Surrounded by the devastation of the war, it was also impossible to ignore the repercussions of his absence. The longer the treaty went unfulfilled, the closer we came to war.

We charged on toward Hagail with only mild trepidation. The road to Oliver was directly through the Thieves' Forest, but I wouldn't allow myself to think about all the dangers that lurked within. It wasn't like we had a choice, at any rate.

Snow started falling once more, and I burrowed further into my cloak. Logan shifted behind me, presumably doing the same.

"Did you hear that?" He pulled on the reins to slow our horse.

"Hear what?"

"Shh." He perked up in the saddle and scanned the copse of trees surrounding our route.

"What is it?" I was starting to get nervous but could neither see nor hear anything that would arouse his suspicion.

Logan didn't answer me, but his arms wrapped more tightly around my waist. With a rough kick, he spurred our horse on. At that same moment, an arrow went whizzing by our heads, snagging on his cloak.

Icy dread filled me as I was hit with the thought that the Aramach had found us. All this time, I had been prepared to face whatever danger came our way to get to Oliver. But I could see clearly the burning bodies of the villagers in my mind, and I wasn't sure that even Logan would be able to win against those savages.

And if we failed, what of my people?

Two horses flanked us as we tried to escape. The assailants grabbed hold of our reins as Logan and I attempted to fight them off. As one of our attackers pulled at me, at least ten more men appeared in the road ahead of us, completely blocking our path.

Ultimately, we were overtaken and came to a complete halt.

"Now, now, now. Ye needn't be alarmed. No one will be hurt, if ye'll only be handin' over yer horse an' valuables." The tall man at the center spoke first.

"Dinna tell 'em tha', Aengus, not when I haven't

decided if I be wantin' tae hurt anyone yet," the man next to him countered.

The one presumably named Aengus playfully shoved the older man in response.

"Aye! I think I'd like to shoot that one between the eyes and maybe have a bit of fun with the other." My head whipped to the right at that, surprised to hear a woman's voice in the group. There, in the tree line with her bow drawn was the cloaked figure who had spoken. She stepped a little closer, never taking her aim off of us. Or me, rather.

I couldn't place her heavy rolling accent as she spoke to him. I wasn't sure I had ever heard someone who sounded like her.

"Imagine all the fun we could have, handsome." The girl tipped her head toward Logan.

My blood boiled with indignation.

"Now, Fia, we've talked about this. We dinna just happily go around murderin' our generous benefactors." Aengus gave the girl named Fia a mocking rebuke.

"Who are you?" The question escaped me as I watched this unanticipated scene unfold. They surely couldn't be the rebels from Bala.

A tall, younger man with skin the color of coal stepped forward, bowing as he spoke. "We are the Ragtag Rebels of Raven Road."

I quirked an eyebrow. If I wasn't so terrified, I'd probably find him handsome.

"No one calls us that, Sai," a small man broke in, his

head barely reaching his friend's waist. "Stop tryin' tae give us names all the time."

"You didn't have to tell them that, Cray." The man called Sai almost sounded hurt.

"We're humble thieves, Milady. Nothin' more. And if ye dinna mind, we'll be gettin' to the theivin' part now." Aengus motioned to the horsemen flanking us, and one of them put a dagger to my throat.

Wonderful. Now they have two methods of killing me in an instant.

The motivation for us to dismount kept us from questioning them further.

We stood still in front of our horse. Despite Logan's skill, there was no way he could overtake this many men. I had faith he could escape, but that was impossible for me, especially with Fia pointing an arrow directly at my head.

"Hand o'er all yer weapons, coin, precious gems, and gold teeth." Cray stepped forward with an open satchel, ready to fill it.

"Err… I don't have any gold teeth." I couldn't believe we were actually being robbed after everything we'd been through.

"Tha's alright, deary," Cray reached up and patted my arm, "Just giv' us yer coin and jewels, then."

Logan motioned for us to hand over the few items on our persons, most of our coin and food being in our horse's satchel. I was grateful Oliver's ring wasn't on my finger, but instead safely tucked away on the delicate chain under my dress. I fought the instinct to grab hold of it, ensuring its safety.

I glanced over as Fia was approaching Logan, finally putting her bow away. She looked every bit the predator advancing on her prey.

"What do you say, lover? Want to come and let me show you a good time?" The presumptuous archer circled him, dragging her finger from his broad shoulders to the middle of his chest.

"I'm afraid I haven't the time, Milady." Logan's words were short, but he almost looked amused by her offer.

"Shame." Fia dragged her finger up and flicked his nose in mock irritation, before turning to face me.

Being this close to her helped me see how young she actually was. The girl couldn't have been any older than Finn. Her hood was pulled low over her face, but I could see her full lips smirking in amusement at whatever she saw on mine.

She was about to speak when something caught her eye. With lightning-fast speed, she reached out and snatched my necklace, snapping the chain.

"No!" I cried out and tried to grab Oliver's ring, but the dagger at my throat dug deeper into my skin.

"Oh, attached, are we? What is this delicious gem I've discovered?" Fia's slender hands threw off her hood and she quickly pawed the ring that I had thought safe.

Without the hindrance of her cloak, I could see the girl fully now. Her long silvery-white locks in stark contrast to her olive skin. One crystal blue and one honey-colored eye peered out from behind her silver lashes. I had never seen such unique beauty before.

I forced myself to refocus on the question she'd just asked, and the item she had stolen.

"It's my wedding ring! Haven't you taken enough already?"

The girl's nimble fingers pocketed the ring so quickly that I barely registered it before she was looming mere inches from my face.

"Careful, Princess." Fia's silver eyebrow quirked, and my heart dropped like lead into my stomach.

Does she know who I am? I was careful to let my features reveal nothing, and she went on after a short pause.

"What good is a pretty little necklace like this without a neck to actually adorn?"

I could hardly contain the rage building within me.

Aengus' voice was loud as he stepped forward, pulling Fia away from me. "Thank ye, truly, fer yer generosity. Now it's time we let ye both continue on yer journey."

"Surely, you wouldn't leave us without a way to defend ourselves." Logan's voice was calm, but his tone was serious as he looked down at Cray, who was merrily absconding with his sword. "After all, there are thieves about."

This earned a laugh from a few of the men before Aengus shook his head and directed the small man back to us.

"Ach! But no' this one! Lookit the helm! Are ye a prince?" Cray turned to beam at Logan, and we both bristled.

Logan's stance relaxed first, and a smirk found its way

to his lips before he spoke. "Ach, no, nothing that exciting. Just won it in a card game against a laird."

"Well, we cannae be partin' with a sword so fine." Cray was determined to keep his new treasure.

"But leavin' 'em without a weapon would be as good as killin' th' missus." One of the other men spoke up in our defense. "Give 'em one o' ours at least."

"Which one? Should we equip him or the lass?"

Fia scoffed. "Look at her. That girl wouldn't be able to tell the tip from the pommel. She clearly doesn't know her way around a sword." She winked.

The thieves laughed at my expense and her double meaning.

Heat rose to my cheeks as I spat out my response. "And it's obvious that you have known your way around many."

I ignored Logan's raised eyebrow and continued to glare at Fia until she finally put her hands up in mock surrender.

The men looked around at each other in shock before a riotous laughter exploded from them.

"Oohh! I like her spirit! Ye better keep this one close to ya, laddie. Or I'll be takin' her for meself!" Cray was doubled over at my brazenly inappropriate retort.

The small man eventually righted himself, went to one of the younger thieves in the company, and removed his sword before bringing it back to Logan.

Luan's Captain studied the blade and worn hilt and shook his head before placing it in his scabbard, clearly unimpressed with the substitution.

"Well, 'tis been a grand ol' time. But we must be on our way. Thank ye for the evenin's entertainments. Be sure tae come back tae donate tae the cause any time."

With that, Aengus and his men disappeared into the snowy forest with all our belongings. Fia turned back, as if one more look at Logan would convince him to run away with her, and laughed as his face remained impassive. She let out a low whistle, and something in the forest stirred in response.

I looked away, unable to bear the sick feeling that overtook me. We had lost every means to get to Oli. We had no horse and no money to buy one. Not to mention, it was late, and we were miles from the last village we'd stopped at.

My hand went absentmindedly to the comfort of Oliver's ring when I pulled up short, feeling nothing but sadness in its place. The weight of its absence was heavier than the ring itself had been. I realized that the only connection I had to him had just been taken, along with any hope I had left.

CHAPTER 25

"Honestly, who makes their way in life by taking other people's belongings?" I grumbled, kicking at a pile of snow. "And who does that wench think she is? Kill me and..." I trailed off.

It was freezing. If we wanted to head back to the village, the trek that had taken us an hour on horseback would take countless more walking. Precious hours that brought us further from any hope of finding Oli or the children. That was if we could even find the path with the way the snow was falling. As such, tempers were short. At least, mine was.

"Perhaps if you hadn't frightened away my horse and refused to secure me another, we wouldn't be in this predicament."

"Yes," Logan's tone was dry, "I'm sure the large band o' thieves that brazenly attacked us on a main road would've been markedly warier had there been a second horse."

I refused to admit the logic of his reasoning.

"What are we supposed to do now?" I pointed around us to the steadily worsening blizzard. I wrapped myself tighter in the heavy wool cloak, pulling my hood lower to ward off the falling snow.

"We walk, Highness. You know, that thing where you use your feet? Commoners do it all the time." Logan's sarcasm snapped the last thread of my temper.

"I'm quite certain you've seen me walk." Then, I registered his renewed use of my title. "Oh, and as long as we're reverting to titles, perhaps I'll start referring to you as Captain Arsehat?" My voice was rising, but I didn't care. "How very familiar, you're treating me like a friend one moment and like a distant monarch the next."

It was getting difficult to see with the white cascading around us.

"You're going to draw unwanted attention." He stiffened, gritting the words through his teeth.

"Indeed, Logan. Perhaps someone will come along and force me to kill them or set fire to a village or steal everything we need to find my fiancé and the kidnapped children! Perhaps they'll throw our two kingdoms into the brink of war!" I threw my hands up. "Honestly, do you think we have a single thing left to lose at this point? Because I'm not too terribly concerned about it myself!"

For a moment, the only sound in the frosty silence was my heartbeat thundering furiously in my ears. Then, Logan's even footsteps crunched away from me. I hurried after him.

"Where are you going?"

"To find us shelter, so we don't freeze to death." His tone was resigned. "But worry not, Highness. You may continue to yell at me while we walk."

I froze, a curious sinking feeling in the pit of my stomach. Had I really expected him to respond to everything I had said? It mattered little, I supposed, with our apparent impending demise on the horizon. I swallowed once and took a deep breath.

The Captain glanced back at me, and I forced my feet to move, one foot in front of the other, trudging through the deep snow. Taking another step forward, I felt the crack before realizing what it was. My foot plunged through the ice and into water, sinking up to my mid-thigh. I yelped, and Logan spun around. He rushed over to me, lifted me out, and set me on the ground. My leg was mostly unscathed, only soaked, and my skirts were sodden.

Logan put both of his hands on my foot and slid them up to my thigh, prodding and assessing along the way. Finally, he gave a grunt. "We need to move. You can't be out in the cold like this. You'll freeze your leg right off."

I shivered and nodded. Standing up, I felt the numbness seep all the way to my toes. I walked after him, the extra weight of my wet, icy dress causing me to lag behind. A thousand hot needles stabbed into my leg, numbness warring the sensation and not quite winning. I stumbled over, hissing in pain.

Logan looked back at me and let out an exasperated groan. He stooped over and lifted me up, his fingers digging into the coldness of my thigh. I held back from crying out, trying not to sound too childish, considering he was already carrying me.

It wasn't hard to see where he was headed, even in the cyclone of snow, the glowing lantern of a farmhouse was shining like a beacon.

The walk was probably shorter than it felt, but between the burning cold in my leg and intensifying shivers, it was as if a lifetime had passed when we finally reached the simple wooden door.

Logan set me down before giving three steady raps on the frame. There was a murmuring of voices before footsteps sounded behind the door.

"What can we do fer ye?" a man's voice intoned through the wood.

I could barely hear him over the wind as it whipped tendrils of icy snow all around and under our cloaks.

"My..." Logan hesitated for only a moment before spitting out the next word. "... *wife* and I were set upon by thieves, and we seek shelter from the blizzard."

Wife. Hearing the word on Logan's lips instead of Oliver's made my heart sink even further into my stomach. I pushed the thought away.

"I'm afraid all we can offer ye is the barn," the man answered. "Times be uncertain an' dangerous people be plenty."

Guilt gnawed at my gut. My people were afraid to open their doors, and we had done nothing to help them.

Father sent men, I reminded myself. He did try.

The howling wind sent snow swirling around us once

more, making the barn sound very appealing. I didn't know how much longer we could be out in this.

"We understand and thank ye, sir." Logan shot me a worried glance. He turned toward the squat building a little way off to the right, then back to me.

He scooped me up once more and headed in the direction of the barn and whatever shelter it might offer. Halfway there, I was startled by a shout. I shifted in Logan's arms to find a tall, older man holding a lantern.

CHAPTER 26

"I can see ye're who you say ye be, an' me wife says t'would be a sin ta leave ye out there in the storm."

Knee-weakening relief chased out every other emotion, and in its wake, a bone-deep weariness.

"Thank you, sir." I fought to talk around my shivers. "We are indebted to you."

"None o' that, lass. Come on, then." He led the way into his modest home.

Logan sat me down gently as soon as we entered into the square, homey space. There was a tiny kitchen in the corner with a low ceiling and what looked to be a room above it. A narrow curtain sat to the left of the crackling fireplace, leading to what I imagined was their bedroom.

A groan escaped my lips when the warmth of the hearth washed over me. No sooner had the door shut behind us than the curtain opened, revealing a white-haired woman in a dressing gown.

"Ach, dearie. Lookit the state o' ye. I told ol' Jimmy we cannae be leavin' ye out there." She moved closer to inspect me.

"We're most grateful," I assured her.

"Yer soaked to the bone, lass." She continued fussing as though I hadn't spoken, placing her hands on my cheeks. "And yer poor cheeks and lips, raw." The woman clucked, shaking her head.

"Bridget, let the lass alone," her husband Jimmy chided.

She moved on to Logan, proclaiming his similarly dire state, then flurried over to the kitchen. Grabbing a bottle of amber liquid, she meted out two generous glasses, pushing one into each of our hands. I took mine gratefully, still fighting back shivers.

"What're yer names, then?" Jimmy asked while his wife headed back into her kitchen.

I opened my mouth to respond, but a yawn came out instead.

"I'm— Craig," Logan interjected. "And my wife is— Blair." There was that word again, and the pang that went with it.

"I'm Jimmy, and me wife o'er there is Bridget. We've no bairns left 'ere in the house, so ye can sleep in their ol' bed." The man pointed up toward the open loft.

"Thank you, again," I said.

Bridget came bustling back over with a small tin of salve she placed into my empty hand and asked her husband to fetch a candle for "Craig."

"Think nothing of it, dearie. Hurry on now." She made a shooing motion with her hands. "Strip out of yer clothes a'fore ye catch yer deaths, an' hand them down tae me. I'll set 'em tae dry by the fire."

I wished I could tell her that wasn't necessary, but it definitely was. Our clothes were sopping wet, and every part of me was freezing. My lower half was somehow raw and numb at the same time. There wasn't a single part of me that didn't ache or chafe with icy dampness.

I decidedly did not look at Logan while I strode toward the ladder leading to the loft we'd be sharing. He stretched up to place a candle and our drinks on the floor of the loft, then he was on my heels. The glow of his candle illuminated the small space and the narrow straw bed in the corner.

For a moment, there was only the sound of our breathing, too loud in the confined space before Bridget called up to us.

"Off with yer clothes then, so I can get them hung."

I picked up my cup, taking a long fortifying sip of my brandy before setting it back down to disrobe. There wasn't much room here for modesty. And, after all, Logan had seen me in my underthings only two days ago. This was no different. Once my dress was off, my hands went automatically to my neck. But of course, Oli's ring wasn't there.

The shuffle of motion and whisper of fabric told me Logan was undressing behind me. I threw my dress and cloak in the general direction I suspected him to be. He sighed when the fabric made impact, but otherwise didn't comment.

I was surprised at the tiny smile tugging at my lips, in

spite of the emotional whirlwind of a day. It was amazing what the hope of being warm could do for a person.

I attempted to avoid looking at Logan in his undergarments, staring at the wall as he spoke to the older woman.

"Truly, thank ye again."

"Dinna fash, laddie. You an' the missus should wrap yerselves up by the fire. No sense in you freezin' to death indoors if the poor girl cannae thaw 'erself. If ye be needin' anythin' at all, jus' give us a knock."

Bridget directed Logan to a small chest at the foot of the bed that contained a stack of blankets. The thought of warmth was more appealing than the dark humor I found in sitting next to the fire in my undergarments, in a stranger's house, with my fiancé's brother.

Wrapping myself up in the dark green blanket from the pile Logan held, I went back down the ladder. Two modest rocking chairs sat in front of the hearth, along with a small table next to each one. A bottle of whiskey, coupled with bread and cheese, sat upon the table closest to the fire, making my choice in seating an easy one.

I made quick work of the small snack before refilling my glass with more delicious spirits. Moving my toes closer to the fire, I finally began to thaw. A tingling sensation crept up my leg as the warmth of the flames soothed my frozen skin.

Each time I closed my eyes, I saw Oliver's face.

What would he make of me in this state?

My chest ached, and my gut felt hollow. Closing my eyes, I took a deep drink of the whiskey. There was nothing I could do in this moment to help him.

I needed to occupy my mind, so it wouldn't dwell on the impossible situation we found ourselves in. My eyes caught on the small bookshelf in the room, and I jumped up to inspect it.

Books had always been important to our family. My father's grandfather had encouraged the people of H'Ria to read and had made sure books were available to nobles as well as the common villagers. Each generation had expanded the literacy programs and edicts in place. H'Ria was a strong kingdom, made only stronger by the education of its people. No matter the political climate and despite the war, that at least had been constant.

The couple had several books I knew, and quite a few that I did not — older tomes with yellowing pages and well-worn bindings. Books that had obviously been loved and passed down through the years. I smiled as I ran my fingers across their leather spines. I wound up choosing a beautiful book with a brown leather cover and small, faded golden font. It looked to be a saga about a lone warrior searching for his love, one I had never read before. I curled up in my chair, ready to enjoy losing myself in the story. But then Logan walked over to join me, disrupting the small measure of peace I'd found for myself.

Pulling the blanket tighter over my shoulders, I attempted to ignore him. I drank more whiskey and stared down at the pages before me. The wording was poetic, and I could immediately see the need to procure a copy for myself. Logan helped himself to more spirits as well. I looked up to see him settling into the chair across from me, wrapped in a warm cream-colored blanket with his own book in hand.

I needn't have worried about him forcing conversation on me. It wasn't his way. He was as content as I was to sip his own beverage and read his book, taking breaks only to look around at every sound. Watching the curtain that concealed the couple's bedroom just in case. *Captain Logan, ever ready and always on alert.*

We stayed this way until the words of the pages became blurry, and I found myself re-reading the same sentence over and over again. The warmth from the fire had finally thawed me enough that I felt I could fall asleep.

I ambled back up to the loft, cocooned in my blanket, and climbed onto the small straw-stuffed mattress, knowing Logan was following me, judging. Despite our silence and our congenial hosts, part of me wondered how much he trusted us in their care. He had been polite, but something in his manner told me he was suspicious.

Logan halted at the top of the ladder, a low groan escaping his lips. He stood still, deliberating. It was my turn to sigh.

I understood his dilemma perfectly. We were both half-naked under our blankets, and the bed was tiny. After everything we had encountered and with the idea of freezing to death still fresh on my mind, it was hard for me to dredge up the energy for propriety. Besides, I was still cold.

"Just come to bed," I said. "We're both exhausted. We'll figure this out in the morning."

It was another few heartbeats before the bed sank next to me, pulling me backward. I clutched my side of the mattress in an effort to keep from rolling into Logan, but he weighed substantially more than I did. I lost my battle for a split second, my backside brushing his hip before I pulled myself back.

He let out a sharp, irritable breath.

"I'm sorry I'm not tiny like those Luanian women you courted," I said, resigned and drained. "If I were, maybe you wouldn't be so uncomfortable sleeping with me in this bed."

Logan was ostensibly silent. My words echoed back to me, the way they did when I'd said something not quite right. A small, mortified giggle escaped my lips when I realized their double meaning. I hadn't been wrong about this trip changing me. I was now apparently an unwitting master of innuendo.

"Stars. I didn't mean it that way," I told him.

He laughed also, but his sounded darker. "Dinna fash yerself. You're of an only average size," he told me in a voice rough with fatigue. "Just get some sleep."

CHAPTER 27

I was reluctant to pull myself out of bed the next morning until an unfamiliar heavy knocking sound finally roused me. While I had been sleeping, I could exist under the pretense of warmth and protection and whispered reassurances. I pulled my mind away from dreams of safety and contentment in my husband's arms.

Will we ever find Oli? Will I ever have that in truth?

The quite literal cold reality of waking in an empty bed in a stranger's house was an abrupt start to my day. Sunlight streamed in through the slats in the closed window, and my clothes sat in a neat pile at the foot of the bed. It had to be late morning.

Why did no one wake me? I threw my dress and cloak on, then opened the latch of the small window.

The world was white, knee-deep snow covering every surface, giant puffy flakes falling fast and swirling angrily with the howling wind. I couldn't see the tree line through the blanket of white, despite knowing it was very near. My heart sank.

How will we make our way to Hagail in this weather?

Jimmy stood in a shoveled-out section of snow, holding up a nail to the roof. Logan's gloved hand reached down for it, and the banging sound commenced.

I closed the window and went down to the main room where Bridget bustled around the kitchen.

"I can't thank you enough for last night," I told her, trying to be grateful for my safety rather than stew in my anxiety for the consequences of being stuck here. Like war.

"Naw, lass. We cannae thank ye enough for lending us yer braw lad," Bridget said, a smile on her aged cheeks. She placed a plate of fried potatoes and eggs on the table, gesturing for me to sit in one of the two chairs. "The roof might have caved right in, if no' fer his help."

I was overwhelmed by the generosity of a couple who clearly had little to spare. The fact that Logan had found a way to repay them in some way made me grateful for his presence, no matter how he'd treated me thus far. It was my fault, after all, for forgetting how he felt about me long enough to let my guard down. If I had expected sympathy from a man who had offered me nothing but condescension for years, I had no one to blame but myself.

I ate quickly and did my best to wash the dishes. I had never actually washed a dish before, but I must have managed, because Bridget didn't outright laugh at me.

Logan was still working away on the roof, so I looked

around for some other way to be of assistance. Knowing little of farm life, I finally swallowed my pride and asked.

"I've got tae get some bread on fer supper, if ye'd like tae help wi' that," she offered.

I nodded, though I hadn't the faintest clue where to begin. It must have shown in my face, because she gave me a kind smile and handed me an apron. She walked over to her rocking chair and sat down, pulling out a pair of her husband's trousers to mend while she talked me through the steps of measuring out ingredients. Her patient tutelage made me wonder if she missed having her children around and where they were now. We didn't seem to be in a hurry, so I asked her.

In between her instructions, she filled me in on the two children she and Jimmy had raised, and how their daughter had married a good man a few miles away. They visited every week with their children. That made me happy, to know this couple wouldn't be out here alone when we left them.

"What about your son? Where did he move?"

"Ach, dearie." Her smile faded and the light dimmed from her eyes as she let her stitching hands rest in her lap for a moment. Her chin quivered just a bit, though she managed to keep her voice mostly steady. "Jack was a braw lad. Much like yer feller." She gave me a soft smile and nodded toward the roof. "He took guid care o' Jimmy and I, he did, until the time came fer him tae join the war."

I hoped against hope that the story wouldn't have the terrible ending my gut was waiting for.

"Jack lasted nigh on six year before he was o'ertaken at the battle of Falam."

She wiped a silent tear that escaped down her nose, before quickly forcing a smile back upon her face. "Ne'er-mind all that, now. We cannae change the past, can we?"

I found myself wiping tears away as well. The realities of the war that still plagued us had never truly affected me. Outside of my betrothal, that was. Her story reinforced my desire to protect my people from ever having to lose their children to such acts of violence again.

We were able to eventually change the somber mood to a happier one as Bridget regaled me with tales of her children's mischief-making youth. Being with her was the most comfortable I had been in a long time. Even though I had no idea what I was doing in the kitchen, the older woman was kind as she taught me my way around a recipe.

It was as if I'd known the matron all my life. By the time the men came in for a noon meal, I was covered in flour and laughing. Logan froze in the doorway, taking me in, from my flour-spattered side braid to the ruffled apron. He shot me an amused smile, and I almost returned it before I remembered how he had treated me the night before.

Instead, I went straight for practicality. "Do we have a plan?" The words came out colder than I had intended, but no more so than his blatant ignorance had last night.

His smile faded. In its wake, purple circles shone prominently underneath his bloodshot eyes. Apparently, I was the only one who had slept the night before.

"We do." His own tone was formal. "I explained the urgency of our situation. Jimmy and Bridget have been so generous as to offer us the use of their horse, provided we return it."

I opened my mouth to argue, but Bridget cut in.

"Oh yes, lass. We dinna need ol' George until the spring at least. Besides, we have our mule Bessie, if there be any need tae leave th' farm."

That had been my concern, so I nodded at her, relieved. Borrowing their horse would solve many problems. The couple truly had no notion of how they had saved us, but I would ensure they were repaid for it.

"When do we leave?" I asked.

He hesitated, and I knew I wouldn't like whatever he was about to say.

"Ach! Ye'll no' be able tae leave yet. I'd venture ye'll be 'ere one mor' night at least," Jimmy interrupted, shaking snow from his boots.

I looked up at Logan for confirmation, and he gave a curt nod of his head. And there it was. The morning with Bridget had been a brief respite from the enormity of our situation, but it came crashing back in on me at that moment. I turned back to knead my dough, letting silence overtake the room.

"Say, how'd the two o' ye meet, then?" Bridget asked.

I supposed it was only fair, her asking personal questions after everything she had shared with me, but it caught me off guard and called to mind things on which I didn't want to dwell.

"I can't really recall," I finally answered, not entirely truthfully. "We've known each other for so long."

"I remember the first time we met," Logan offered.

My hands froze, knuckles inches deep into the dough, but I didn't turn around.

"I was ten, and you were eight." He turned to Bridget and Jimmy. "I was the new lad in town, an' there were many who didn't accept me. But Blair," he stumbled only a little over the name he had given me, "looked at me without a trace o' judgment. She stuck out her hand, almost as big as mine back then." He chuckled, and I resisted the urge to glare at him. I towered over tiny Bridget by a solid foot. My size was hardly a secret.

"She said, 'Welcome to the family.' And with that single edict, Blair made that first summer bearable, she and our other friends."

I didn't remember saying that, but I remembered what had come next.

"I'm Logan," the boy said.

"I'm Charlotte, and this is my brother Finnian. But we all call him Finn."

"Finn." Logan nodded. "It suits you."

My brother beamed.

"You, though." The redheaded boy examined me for a moment. "You don't look like a Charlotte. I think we should call ye Charlie."

The memory stung, and I shook it off.

"Yes," I resumed my kneading. "Growing up... where we did, it was easy to feel alone. We were fortunate enough to make our own small family, a group of friends who understood each other, who we could confide in and commiserate with. Until that changed, of course." I let the woman interpret that how she would. Logan would know precisely what I meant, how he had abandoned our family without explanation.

He didn't react at all. There was another beat of silence before Jimmy launched into a story of how he met his wife. It was an adorable tale of young love, and tears pricked my eyes. For so long, I had known exactly where my life was going. I pictured Oli and I telling our grand-children of the treaty, how our love and union had strengthened two countries, staved off a war. A couple of tears tracked unbidden down my cheeks, and I prayed I had enough kneading to keep me turned around until they dried up.

CHAPTER 28

After lunch, Logan and Jimmy went back out to finish patching the leak in the roof.

Bridget continued with her stitching while I nestled into the same blanket with the same book and began reading next to her by the fire. We stayed in a companionable silence until it was time to prepare supper.

Kneading bread was one thing, but I felt a little overwhelmed at my ineptitude when it came to cooking. Nevertheless, I was curious to learn, and to be useful in whatever way possible.

An array of ingredients sat before us on the kitchen table: venison, some assorted pickled vegetables, seasonings like rosemary and fennel, a salt brick, and peppercorns. I hadn't the faintest idea how they would become a meal.

Under the older woman's careful tutelage, I set to work. For as long as I could remember, every meal had been provided for me. This was the first time I prepared anything by myself.

The rhythm we fell into felt natural. It was all unexpectedly soothing, meting out ingredients and carefully combining them. In a different life, I imagined I would have loved to be the one to do this for my family. To take simple ingredients and form them into a meal. To mix and combine and season and create something that my family would need but also enjoy.

I lost myself in my work, humming along to one of my favorite songs. Bridget smiled at me, lending a beautiful whistling melody to the tune. As much as I had loved my life, I couldn't help but envy the woman's daughter in this moment.

I pondered my relationship with my own mother. I knew life on her home island of Divalis had been a simpler one, but at Castle Chridhe, there had never been time for learning lessons such as these. Governesses and tutors had instructed me in etiquette, languages, politics, music, and embroidery. The most time I spent with my parents together was our one day a week in the throne room.

After putting the main dish into the oven, we started on dessert. Bridget brought over some canned apples from the pantry, along with a small jar of honey, eggs, and more flour. She directed me in making the dough needed for a pastry crust. With each swipe of the rolling pin, I imagined myself living this simpler life. And I loved it.

When it finally came time for us all to sit together at the table, there was a comfortable exhaustion that overtook me along with a sense of pride for what we had accomplished.

The men smiled at the meal spread out in front of them. Without a moment's hesitation, they served us and then themselves. Everyone dug in, conversation halted until we had all sufficiently stuffed ourselves. I savored the moment, pleased that it had turned out so well.

"This is delicious, ma'am. I don't know if I've ever had roasted venison this fine." Logan grinned around another mouthful of food.

"Ach! I imagine ye have! Since it be yer wife that made it!" Bridget gave me a wink as she said this, grinning as she passed another helping to her husband. "Or I imagine ye'll at least enjoy it again. It is delicious, lass. Ye be a mighty fine cook."

I ignored Logan's raised eyebrows, pretending it was completely natural that I should be a good cook.

I couldn't help but wonder what Oliver would have thought of me doing work such as this. Would he have been proud of my accomplishment today? Merely confused? Would I ever find out?

I did my best to keep up my end of the conversation, but even the satisfaction I had gotten from cooking managed to ebb away. By the end of the meal, Logan was taking the brunt of the conversation with Jimmy and Bridget.

AFTER DINNER, LOGAN AND JIMMY WENT OUT TO SEE TO the animals. I stared into the fireplace, willing my thoughts to disintegrate the way the wisps of smoke did. Bridget, with all the instincts of a mother, came to put an arm around me.

"It'll be al'right, dearie. Marriage t'will always be difficult a'first, but as long as ye're with the person ye love, it has a way o' workin' itself out. Ye'll see."

That's the problem, isn't it? I stepped out of her embrace before I succumbed to threatening tears. I finished up the dishes, then excused myself to go to bed. It was early yet, but I was drained. And as much as I appreciated Bridget's company, I wanted to be alone.

I stripped off my clothes to just my underthings. Logan wouldn't see me under the blanket, and I wasn't ready to part with having a moderately unrumpled dress just yet. No sooner had I crawled into bed than the tears I had held at bay began falling freely. I cried for the villagers at Bala and the missing children. I cried for Oli and myself and the gut-wrenching loneliness I couldn't seem to dispel, the hollow feeling of longing for things I was starting to wonder if I would ever have.

The floorboard gave a quiet creak. *Blasted stars.* I tried to even out my breathing, but I only succeeded in taking a couple of shuddering breaths before my shoulders shook again. I covered my face with my hands. Logan hadn't said anything or moved since climbing up the ladder, so maybe he would just ignore me.

I couldn't seem to get my tears under control, but at least I managed to muffle them. Perhaps Logan didn't notice. Seconds later, though, his weight pulled the other side of the bed down.

I expected him to put his usual amount of distance between us, but he settled against my back and his solid arm wrapped around me in a gentle hug. The unexpected gesture only made my silent tears come faster.

He didn't ask me what was wrong, didn't speak at all. I didn't offer an explanation, instead taking what little comfort I could from the nearness of my old friend. Even if he would go back to hating me tomorrow, I was grateful some part of him cared enough to give me this.

CHAPTER 29

I was relieved, upon awakening, that Logan had spared us both the awkwardness of waking up together after he had witnessed me falling apart the night before. I dressed and emerged from the room in time to help with breakfast while Logan was out shoveling snow.

I made polite conversation with Bridget and Jimmy while we ate, studiously avoiding Logan, and he seemed content to reciprocate. By the time we finished breakfast, the snow had let up just enough for us to see the main road and the tree line behind it. Our gracious hosts had offered for us to stay one more night. As much as I had enjoyed my time with the sweet couple, urgency drove us forward. Those children needed us, and Oli was waiting.

Logan saddled the couple's horse, George, thanking them again. I had one foot in George's stirrup when Bridget stopped me. Setting the worn green blanket I'd come to love into my arms, she placed a motherly kiss upon my cheek. Surprised tears welled up at the gesture.

"Such a bonnie lass." She patted my hand as she smiled up at me. "Ye take guid care o' this one, lad."

Logan nodded to the older lady, assuring her he would do his best.

Reaching out, I hugged the couple once more and made a silent promise that I would return one day, hopefully soon. We would need to return George to them along with a gift for their generosity. But part of me wanted to come back just for the comfort of the small home and the kindness within it.

After being plied with handfuls of salted meats and bread and canteens of water, they finally sent us on our way. I resisted the urge to dig my heels further into the plow horse. He would never reach the speed of the war destrier we had borrowed from Laird Ewan, but he also wouldn't draw attention.

We had no choice but to head into the Thieves' Forest blind, hoping we weren't set upon again, and pray we could find a way to make camp. My father's men were still days away, if he had even gotten the message we sent.

Will Oli still be in Hagail when we finally make it?

I couldn't think that way. Not if I wanted to keep my composure. Logan was rigid at my back, keeping as much space between us as possible. That was fine by me. I didn't have the energy to pretend we were anything more than two strangers who used to be friends, forced on a journey to rescue someone we both loved. I appreciated last night, but I didn't expect him to behave any differently than usual this morning.

I bit back a bitter laugh. Logan remembered the day our friendship formed surprisingly well. My most vivid memories were of the day it ended.

The summer I turned fifteen, Logan had started his training to be Captain of the Guard. After that day on the lake, he had been sent on a short tour. The four of us had been so worried, especially Oli. I had stayed up late with him every night that week, trying to offer what little comfort I could.

Seven days later, we finally received word that Logan was home safe, but he made no move to visit any of us.

I could still remember my little brother's pinched features when he asked Oliver why Logan, who up until that point had been Finn's hero, hadn't bothered to let us know he was home. Oli had shrugged and said something noncommittal about Logan being busy with his training, but I could see a trace of that hurt reflected in his eyes also.

The day before I left, I finally sought Logan out in the training room. He was alone, sword in hand, facing off against some invisible foe. His brow gleamed with sweat and the laces of his training shirt were coming loose, but I didn't care about any of that.

I called his name to get his attention. He looked up, startled, and froze. For a moment, I felt as though he stared straight through me. Then, he seemed to register who I was.

"Highness." Logan's tone was more resigned than surprised to see me.

I looked around, but the room was empty.

"Charlie," I corrected him.

He looked away. "Don't you think it's time to let that go? We aren't children anymore. It isn't proper."

"To the stars with propriety," I said, a little taken aback by the surge of anger that shot through my veins. "What is this really about? Why haven't you come to see Finn or me? We're leaving tomorrow."

"Contrary to your beliefs, Highness, the world does not revolve around your comings and goings. Some of us have responsibilities." His eyes sparked with anger, but it was nothing compared to my own.

"Right, and I would know nothing about that, what with being a future queen!" I spat the last word at him.

I had stormed out, half expecting him to seek me out sometime later that day to apologize. We had been prone to our share of heated debates, but we had never actually fought, not like this. Even when I pushed him in the lake, he had laughed it off.

But he never sought out Finn or me. We left the next day. By the time I saw Logan nearly a year later, it was as if we had never been friends at all. Things were never the same after that. Isla and Finn still talked, and me and Isla. Of course, Oli and I were close as ever, but the dynamic of our makeshift family was gone.

It was only now, looking back, that I wondered if we should have fought harder for Logan. I wasn't an idiot. He had told me only two days ago about the first time he saw carnage like that at Bala. That day he had distanced himself had been the day he'd come home broken from warfare. It was clear why he had pulled away.

Had he confided in anyone? Oliver, even?

A terrified scream pulled me from my reverie. It was too high, even for a woman's voice. My blood ran cold.

Logan cursed behind me, dismounting the horse with blurring speed. He looked up at me.

"This may be a trap, but I need to go. If you see any danger, ride as fast as this horse will carry you back to the farmhouse."

"I'm not going to leave you here, Logan."

"Yes, you are—" He started to argue, but another high-pitched wail interrupted him.

"All right. Of course. Whatever you say. Just go! It's a child, Logan." My voice was panicked.

He took off into the woods. The sound of his boots crunching through the icy snow lingered, even as I lost sight of his cloaked form behind a large hill. I debated following, but I knew I would only slow him down.

My mind flitted to the female archer we had encountered just two days ago. When we finally made it home, I was determined to learn the bow as well. Perhaps I would never be as good as the girl they'd called Fia, but I was determined to never find myself in a position where I could not help again. So, I forced myself to stay put, alert and searching for any danger.

It was only seconds later that I heard Logan's roar. The voice of another man rang out, followed by the clashing of steel. Raised, panicked voices carried on through the quiet midday air. I clutched the reins, my stomach in knots, as I tried to make out what they were saying.

Is Logan outnumbered? Should I go after him? How could I help him escape?

The sounds of the fighting abruptly ceased. I knew Logan was an unparalleled warrior, but that didn't stop me from worrying about his fate. After an interminable stretch of silence, crunching footsteps drew near.

The Captain had returned, but he wasn't alone.

He was with the band of thieves.

CHAPTER 30

"What is this?" I looked at Logan for any signs of duress but found none.

The leader, Aengus, walked with his arm companionably around the Captain's shoulders. A smile graced both faces, though Logan's was a bit more hesitant than the older man's.

"Yer lad here is a braw lad! A hero!" Aengus beamed at me as the other men shouted their approval.

The look of surprise and hesitation must have been plain on my features. Logan met my eyes, giving me a nod of approval, and I forced myself to relax a little.

"Ye shoulda seen him!" Cray was animatedly reenacting the display he'd borne witness to, thrusting his invisible sword through the air. "Mak' no mistake, Rheisart's men'll think twice afore comin' after us again."

Another man, who I recognized as being one of the horsemen that had stopped us that infamous night, was carrying a boy in his arms. The child couldn't have been more than eight or nine years old. They both looked at Logan with nothing but respect and revere in their eyes.

"Thank ye, truly." Tears glistened in his eyes. "I dinna ken what I'd have done if… If ye'd not made it to him in time. Yer owed a debt, friend."

"Ach, Neacal, the boy is safe now. Ye needn't make a fuss." Despite Cray's admonishment, the spritely man looked as if he was rife with emotion as well. "Rheisart's the devil himself these days. His men be havin' no compunction between 'em. No more honor in the whole lot."

What an interesting group of men. They didn't at all fit the frightening descriptions of the thieves we'd always been warned about. The kind that, apparently, this Rheisart was becoming.

The men continued their tale of Logan's saving act. Apparently Neacal's son was a scout for the band. He had ventured too far from the camp's borders and run into a few of the hunters for this other troupe of thieves. Evidently, the group had been more protective of their borders over the past few months, violating the long-existing truce among their fellows.

The child hadn't come back to camp long after he should've returned, so his family had set out to find him. Their rivals found them first, however. They had been taunting the boy from the bottom of the tree he was hiding in, forcing him to stay up in the safety of its branches. When they finally managed to dislodge him, their relentless blows were cruel and intentional. By the time Logan had reached them, one of the men had a dagger out and was beginning to carve into the boy's skin.

I had shivered at their retelling. The stories I'd heard as a child about the Thieves' Forest made sense listening to the morbid tale. This was the sort of reputation Dorcha was known for.

Logan hadn't hesitated when he discovered the scene. According to those men, he immediately leapt upon the one inflicting the most damage, knocking him out cold. The other had produced a sword behind him but was nowhere near as skilled as Logan. They had dueled for a short time before his assailant gave up and fled, abandoning his companion entirely when the child's family arrived to help.

"Well t'would seem that maybe we misjudged ye. Ye not be jus' the typical nobles who dinna care abou' us commoners. Thank ye kindly." Aengus reached out to shake Logan's hand, a sincere look of gratitude on his face.

"The Burglars of The Bleak Boscage are indebted to you." The dark young man named Sai bowed to us.

"Stop yer confuse' way o' speakin', Sai! We dinna have a name and if we did t'would never be one like that!" Cray punched a discouraged-looking Sai in the arm.

"Why dinna ye just come on back tae camp wi' us? 'Tis gettin' late and ye nae be wantin' tae find yerselves in these woods at night." Aengus motioned us toward the copse of trees on our left. There was a small path that I hadn't noticed earlier leading back into the dense forest.

"We really need to reach Hagail. Urgent matters take

us there, and we cannot be delayed any longer. But thank you for your kind offer." I was grateful for Logan's response, as I couldn't imagine waiting any longer to get to Oli.

"Nonsense, laddie! Hagail 'tisn't a place tae underestimate. Ye nah be wantin' tae find yerselves there in the dark. The lowest kind o' folks prowl the ol' towne. Anyway, there be worse bands o' thieves in these woods than we.

'Tisn't safe tae go any further by moonlight, not now that ye've made enemies. Nay, we cannae let ye go on. Come with us." Aengus' tone was insistent. "We'll take ye to th' blasted towne tomorrae. Make sure ye get there safely."

I looked down at Logan and watched as he deliberated for a moment, considering the pros and cons of our situation. After our delay in leaving Bridget and Jimmy's, and again here in the forest, it would be well into the early hours of the morning by the time we reached Hagail if we left right then. That was only if we weren't set upon by even more thieves. Thieves like Rheisart's men, who might leave us without more than just our possessions, more likely without our heads.

I swallowed hard, following the line of thinking I knew Logan was debating as well and came to the same conclusion just as he looked up at me. With a quick nod of his head, he signaled his consent. I wasn't happy about having to stop so soon, but I knew they were right. So I nodded as well and thanked the men for their offer.

Aengus motioned toward the path once more. "Come

on then. We'll give ye back yer horse an' other *donations,* too."

His use of the term 'donations' made Logan chuckle dryly as he climbed up behind me on George.

"Lead the way," he told them.

CHAPTER 31

It was exactly like a faerie story. The light from the fire in the middle of camp illuminated the trees in a way that was both haunting and magical. Children ran and laughed between small make-shift cabins as the enticing aroma of supper and spiced wine permeated the air. Musicians twirled around the flames along with the dancers. And a woman sang a swift refrain about a man gone to sea to find his true love.

Isla would love this.

The clearing that was the thieves' home was a warm and merry place that enraptured and bewildered me. Despite the blizzard, there was little snow here. The dense canopy of the forest formed a shelter, seemingly just for them. Several of the men had referred to this place as a 'camp,' but it was more like a secret village, a small oasis.

I dismounted George, leaving him to the care of Sai, the camp's self-appointed horseman. A glance at Logan told me that he was just as taken by this place as I was.

Pleased, I smiled at the scene before me, until familiar guilt gnawed at my stomach.

Will we never find Oliver?

I let out a deep sigh and allowed Cray and Aengus to herd me farther into the camp. Logan and I were given a small tent to share for the evening. I reluctantly placed the soft, worn quilt that Bridget had gifted me inside of it, along with the satchel of food they'd sent with us. I smiled as I thought of their kindness.

I left the tent behind to wander the campsite, finding comfort in the way the people enjoyed themselves. A few young lovers had found a cozy place by the flames and were nestled into one another, speaking in hushed tones. I averted my eyes, shaking off the unwelcome feelings the sight wrought within me.

To my left, several people gathered to hear Neacal recount what happened to his son. A few older women listened along as they fussed over the child, busying themselves with bandaging his wounds and stuffing him with food.

Never in my life would I have expected to see such... normality... here in the forest. My mind reeled with the tales I had heard and the reality before me. I wondered, not for the first time, why they made their living as thieves when their nature seemed to be so at odds with it.

I made my way over to introduce myself to the boy, whose name I learned was Avery. His wounds weren't overly serious, but they weren't something to shake off, either. Overall, he seemed to be suffering more from the embarrassment of having been caught than his actual wounds. I sat and spoke with him for a while until I finally saw a smile spread across his face.

"They do?" Avery asked, reaching up to touch the cut on his forehead.

"Really. Girls love a boy with scars. Shows how strong he is. You're a regular warrior now." I smiled back at him and nudged him a bit with my shoulder. "You should never be ashamed of your scars. That's the proof you have of surviving the monsters who thought they were stronger than you."

Avery stared at me wide-eyed before looking back to his mother for confirmation. She nodded and rubbed his cheek, tears brimming in her eyes.

I eventually made my excuses, giving the boy a small peck on the forehead as I said goodbye, reminding him, again, of how brave he had been. His cheeks reddened, but he sat up a little taller when his friends ran over to check on him.

As I walked away, I no longer saw the dispirited injured boy that had been sitting there before. In his place sat a warrior, proud of his battle scars and the tale he'd lived to tell.

At least this is one child I can help.

The morose thought took the wind from my sails once more. This must have been obvious on my features, because Cray approached, grabbed me by the arm, and delivered me to their jovial leader before disappearing once more.

"Ye need tae eat, lass. That'll help put a smile back on yer face." Aengus thrust a bowl filled with a delicious smelling stew into my hands. "Me wife makes the best bread. Here, take some more." My mouth watered at the sight before me. It did, in fact, both look and smell wonderful.

Cray returned with a mug of warm hypocras that he swore would take my mind off of my worries.

If only he knew.

"Is it like this every night?" I gestured to the joyous crowd.

"Oi wish! But 'tis only the Winter Festival, lass." The small man could barely contain the effect the music was having on him. He gave me a toothy grin as he spun in time with the melody. In all of the chaos, my favorite celebration had slipped my mind entirely. I thanked Cray for my drink as he scurried off to join in the dancing.

My heart was in a state of confused sadness as I took in the revelry. This was the time to be with family, but where was mine? I had left my parents at Castle Chridhe. My brother was injured. I was grateful for the knowledge that Isla was by his side. Oli was... I was on my way to my fiancé, but I could barely bring myself to consider the circumstances he was in at the moment.

And what of my people? Would they be celebrating Winter Festival with their families next year, or out needlessly sacrificing their lives?

I sat down on a log bench near the fire, hoping that the meal in my hands would calm the bleakness overtaking me.

It was exactly the momentary distraction I'd needed. Each bite was more delicious than the last. I used the warm bread to scoop up every last morsel, scraping it against the sides and not wasting a single drop. When I looked up from my empty bowl, several of the camp's children were surrounding me. Apparently, they had been admonished to leave me be until I was finished with my meal. They hadn't waited a second longer.

I couldn't help but smile at them as they peppered me with one question after another. As much as I was enjoying their presence, I hated myself for not being able to be completely honest with them about who I was. It was hard to remember the pretense I was supposed to keep when staring into the innocent eyes of ones so young.

Two girls pushed their way to the front of the group holding a wreath made of dried leaves, thistles, and winter berries. After placing it upon my head, the girls beamed.

"Ach, lookit 'er! She looks jus' like a princess!"

I kept my face neutral, biting back a laugh. If only they knew.

"A faerie princess!" The girls giggled as they admired their handiwork. I couldn't help but giggle a little back at them as they skittered off to pass out more of their creations.

The adults started to dance in a clearing under the hanging lanterns. I was surprised to see the steps weren't so different from those in the court dances, just performed with fewer inhibitions.

The children were forced to say their good-nights when their parents came to herd them away, muttering apologies. Of course, I hadn't minded. I had enjoyed my time with them, the reprieve from constantly guessing at someone else's motives. I watched as the families all resumed their dancing, together this time.

The children had been a guileless distraction. Once they were gone, I was left with my own thoughts once more.

I imagined the children from Bala. It was so hard to not know what was happening to them. Their parents were no longer alive like the parents here. There was no one to love them, to remind them when to eat. No one to scold them when they teased their siblings or to tuck them in at night.

They were not safe. They were not warm. They were stolen away by the monsters who slaughtered their families.

I shook my head, pressing the heels of my hands to my eyes, trying to push the thoughts from my mind. The music's tempo was picking up for a faster dance. I tried to make myself feel the happiness that abounded in each note.

CHAPTER 32

Someone sat down next to me, easing right up to my side, despite the ample room on the log. I glanced up, surprised to find Logan holding a mostly-empty stein of the warm hypocras.

I raised my eyebrows, unwilling to speak first as I was unsure of what to say. We hadn't spoken more than a few perfunctory sentences since his story at the farmhouse. Logan looked at me for only a second before turning to face the clearing. I followed his gaze, staring at the twirling, laughing mass without really seeing it.

Finally, he cleared his throat.

"It isn't like you to not be out there," he said.

I deliberated for a moment before responding. "And it isn't like you to care what I'm doing."

I went to take another sip of my spiced wine and was surprised to find it empty. Perhaps that was why I wasn't as cold as I had been earlier.

I held my hand out for Logan's stein. He handed it

over with surprisingly little objection, watching me take several long sips before returning it to him. He drained the remaining liquid and stood up in a single, fluid movement.

Features carved into neutrality, he held a broad, calloused palm out toward me. I stared up at him questioningly. I knew Logan could dance. I had witnessed him dancing with every girl at court over the past several years, but he always ended the night by complaining about the necessity of it and missing his years living in a village where no one kept a careful rote of everyone he had danced with that week.

"You hate dancing," I said, not yet taking his hand.

"I never said that." He stood as steady as the trees around us. "It's been a hell of a week, Charlie. There's nothin' more we can do at the moment. Would it really be the worst thing in the world to forget it all for a few moments?"

When he puts it that way...

I looked over to the dancers and realized I wanted nothing more than to be in their midst, letting the wine and the music and the magical forest take me away. I placed my hand in his.

Logan led me to the middle of the clearing, earning shouts of approval from the men that we were finally joining them. We both chuckled as we stepped in line to the choreographed dance.

When was the last time I danced with Logan?

At the Luanian Court, dancing was expected nearly every night, accompanied by their Court Minstrel. Logan had always made up his own lyrics to her ridiculous songs, singing them under his breath during our dances. It had been all I could do to keep from laughing under the ever-critical eye of Queen Siobhan.

Of course, that had been back when we were friends and Logan actually smiled occasionally.

It wasn't long before my thoughts dissolved into the sparkling night air. Slow turns and quick steps had us making use of the entire space, each set of dancers swaying and mingling before switching partners.

I focused on the words of the beautiful song. Each note carried a message of honesty and hope. Of burying toes in the sand by the riverbed and flying away with the one you love. One by one, the words reverberated within my heart.

Somewhere between the warmth of the wine and the fire, the encompassing thrum of the music and the lanterns spinning over my head with each twirl, I felt like I could breathe again. Towering trees swayed above us as if they were dancing along. It was enchanting.

The slower song morphed into a faster, jauntier tune, the kind of dance where one changed partners frequently. The kind that wouldn't allow me to think about anything but the next step and the next twirl. I was spun from Logan to Sai, then Cray, then to a series of unfamiliar faces. I held fast to my crown with one hand, laughing as each spin threatened to topple it.

Any worry that the unfamiliar men might try their luck was quickly dispelled. I had been subjected to more impropriety at court than I was receiving in the Thieves' Forest.

Usually from Oli, I thought wryly.

The dancing picked up tempo, yet again. My twirling feet hardly touched the ground. Laughter bubbled unabated from my lips when the man I was dancing with turned me over to my next partner with a bit too much vigor.

Strong arms caught me, setting me aright. I looked up into Logan's amused face, my jaw dropping when his rumbling laughter reached my ears.

When was the last time I heard him laugh like this? Has anyone?

The music finally crested before transitioning back into a calmer composition once more, which was fortunate, since I was beginning to pant from the effort of keeping up with the other. My eyes drifted to the left hand resting on Logan's shoulder with its conspicuously unadorned fingers.

"Do you honestly think we'll find him, Logan?" I was afraid of what his answer would be, but the wine was forcing me to address our inescapable reality.

His shoulders slackened as he let out a sigh. "I truly hope so."

I looked away from the grief I saw in his eyes, focusing instead on the lanterns above us. I tried not to think of the way my hand fit in Oliver's. I tried not to think of the way he would smile at me or how his eyes sparkled when he was planning something mischievous. I tried not to compare my dance with his brother, with the way Oliver had swept me across the floor. Or how he always pulled me a little too close for propriety's sake, just to make a scene.

The song came to an end. Exhaustion from both the dancing and a week of emotional upheaval made me feel threadbare.

"I think I need another drink." I looked up at Logan, and he nodded his agreement.

CHAPTER 33

W e grabbed our cups and walked toward the giant pot of the brew suspended over a lightly crackling fire.

"Bes' swordsman oi e're seen!" Cray was recanting the rescue from earlier, his hands moving rapidly to showcase the skill he had witnessed.

The children who were still awake listened to the tale, enraptured. They stared at Logan as we passed, awe covering their glowing features next to the fire.

There was a reason he had been the youngest person to ever be appointed Captain of the Guard. He had always been stronger than the other boys, but it was his quick mind that made him an unparalleled opponent.

Once we reached the kettle of the delicious mulled wine, Logan ladled out a large portion into my cup, much to my delight. He was moving on to his own when Fia slinked up to us, flipping something across her knuckles.

At first, I thought it was a coin. Then the light of the

fire caught on what was clearly a cluster of pearls and diamonds. The wench had my ring. My eyes narrowed, and she smirked.

"Stand down, Princess. I was coming to return your precious ring. It's not my style, anyway," she added with a toss of her long white blonde curls.

I rolled my eyes, but took the delicate gold band, sliding it into place on my third finger, now that I had no chain upon which to place it.

"Where's yours?" She looked at Logan, but something in her tone told me she knew perfectly well we weren't married.

I didn't think the thieves would betray us after accepting us into their sanctuary. Besides, I was tired of lying about everything. Logan opened his mouth to answer her, likely with a fabrication, but I cut him off.

"Logan and I aren't married. He's practically my brother, actually. We're only out here together because he's helping me find my husband." I ignored the irritable look Logan shot at me. It was a relief to get the words out. I wasn't accustomed to having to keep track of so many falsehoods.

Her feral grin was unsurprised. "Indeed." Fia eyed Logan like he was a prize-winning stallion, running her hand over his chest in much the same manner. "In that case, join me for a dance." She pulled him along behind her with surprising force, given her size, not that he resisted.

I debated heading back to the clearing, but the high from the dancing had largely worn off. Instead, I trudged back to the tent they had given us earlier, wine in tow. The way the lights filtered through the green canvas brought to mind the enormous tree I had often escaped to at Oli's castle.

Despite my best efforts to behave, I had never quite managed to quell my tendency to sneak out into the woods when I needed a moment alone. A princess' life was rarely solitary. Among those trees had been the only place I could find peace.

Through the summer visits, there were times the five of us would sneak out, but I always picked a different spot for those outings. There underneath the protective branches of the willows had been mine alone, until that summer when I was fifteen.

One night, when Logan was gone on tour and Finn crept off to see Isla, I told Oli to meet me in the gardens. I was so nervous, I could hardly speak when he asked me where we were going. I grabbed his hand and tugged him behind me until we got to my tree.

"Where are we going, love?" Oli looked around, chiseled features screwed up with confusion.

My heart fluttered each time he called me that.

"We're here. This is my favorite tree." The nervousness I felt at showing him this part of me warred with the anxiety of being so alone with him for the first time.

"You have a favorite tree?" He sounded bewildered. "How can you tell it apart from the other trees?"

I laughed and shook my head, ducking under the low-hanging branches. He followed me into the space underneath, and I leaned back against the trunk on trembling legs. Now that we were here, I wasn't sure how to continue. But Oli was no one's fool.

He had kissed me before, light pecks on the lips in stolen moments. This time was different, however. He put his warm lips on mine, letting them rest there for a moment before pulling back. I followed him, not ready for the sensation to end.

He let out an eagerly appreciative groan and put his hands around my waist, pulling me closer to him. The movement put me off balance, and we wound up tumbling over, sprawled on the ground. Under the branches of my willow tree, it was easy to feel like we were in another world, one where propriety didn't exist. Where there was no one else but Oli and me.

I didn't bother sitting back up, instead allowing Oli to run his hands over my body while he intensified his kisses. His hands trailed lazily from my back to my waist, cupping my hip before moving on toward my thigh.

He pulled back and smirked, pleased to be able to explore more of me than he had before.

"I think I have a favorite tree now also, love." His fingers intertwined in mine as his eyes raked over me.

I giggled, my body shaking with the intensity of the moment. We lay there, secluded from the rest of the world, for what seemed like forever.

One of the dancers squealed with laughter, pulling me back into the present. The small space in my tent felt empty after the vivid recollection of Oli. My stomach was knotted in anxiety, and sleep felt further away than the stars above. Tomorrow could be the day we got my husband back, and I wouldn't be able to face it without sleep. I drained the last dregs of my wine, using it to push out the noises of the revelry and my own churning thoughts until I finally drifted off.

———

MY EYES FLEW OPEN. I TOOK A MOMENT TO GET MY bearings, trying to discern what had startled me. The noises of the revelry had largely died down, so I didn't think that was it. Unable to shake off the feeling, I got to my feet and poked my head out of the canvas. Logan's redheaded form was walking away from the tent.

Has he forgotten something?

I opened my mouth to ask him when a rich feminine laugh reached my ears. Fia leaned against a tree next to her cabin, smirking at Logan. Once he was close enough, she grabbed his hand and all but yanked him into her cabin.

It appeared I hadn't been far off with my assessment of her character that first day.

CHAPTER 34

My head was spinning. Between the large amounts of wine I'd had and the evening of fitful sleep, I felt terrible. The entire night had passed between drifting into reluctant sleep and anxious awakenings, alone in the frigid air. I was nothing short of relieved when it was finally over.

I left the tent, aware of my unkempt state, desperate to find out if tea or coffee was available. Aengus' wife milled about the camp, readying breakfast for everyone. She laughed as she took in my appearance and pointed to the kettle over the fire. My brow furrowed in confusion, but then the enticing scent of coffee wafted over to me.

I took a few small sips of the deliciously strong brew as I absorbed the camp in the light of day. Even without the twinkling lanterns, it was no less magical. Brilliant rays of sun streamed in from the canopy above, showcasing the small hamlet the thieves had made for themselves.

There were even more cabins than I had realized, some larger than others. The children were already up and running around, imitating the moves they'd seen Cray display the night before. The young scout from yesterday proclaimed himself to be Logan, and I had to bite back a laugh. I imagined he would be admired here for quite some time.

Speak of the devil.

I took a long sip from my mug as I watched the man himself emerge from a cabin straight across from me, followed directly by that minx, Fia.

The catlike woman looked at me and winked, clearly pleased with her conquest. Judging by the bags under his eyes, Logan hadn't gotten any more sleep than I had, though for vastly different reasons. He gave me an awkward nod, and I returned it with raised eyebrows, giving him a mocking salute with my coffee cup. I had never known the man to be free with his affections at court, but perhaps things were different for a soldier on the road.

In any event, it was hardly my business.

"When do we head out?" I asked no one in particular.

"Soon." Aengus was striding toward Logan with a smile and his original sword in hand. "We dinna burglarize from our own. Ye'll get yer horse back, too." He turned back to me and winked. "Here's yer coin as well, lass. Mighty generous o' ye tae lend tae the cause, but we needn't be keepin' yer donations after all." He dropped a small bag with the funds they'd pilfered only three nights ago.

I chuckled at his description of what had happened. Lending and donating weren't the terms I'd use for being robbed.

"We'll leave a'soon as we load up th' horses." Aengus began to saddle his own mount as he spoke.

It was all the incentive I needed to race back to my tent. I packed up our few belongings. *Will this all be over soon?* My stomach churned violently with anticipation and fear.

I hadn't really gotten anything out of the small satchel to begin with, so it was just a matter of folding our borrowed blanket. I was gathering the ends uncertainly when Logan walked in the tent.

"Need any help?"

I shot him an irritable look over my shoulder.

"I know how to fold a blanket." I didn't, but I could figure it out.

"All right then." He left as quickly as he had come.

I emerged a moment later, lopsided blanket over my shoulder. Logan glanced at me, and I dared him with a look to comment on it. He wisely refrained, turning his attention back to Fia instead.

Sai came to take my pack and blanket, which he refolded without comment before securing both items to the laird's horse. Fia sauntered over as I was mounting my horse. She pulled out a dagger, her face inscrutable.

Is she going to use that?

But she surprised me by flipping it around and handing it to me hilt first.

"You're giving this to me?" I asked, hesitantly reaching for the blade.

"So you won't be completely useless." She smirked, tossing a belt at me before turning to go.

Of course.

"Besides," Fia called over her shoulder, "it reminded me of you."

My brow furrowed while I examined the jeweled dagger. It had a siren carved onto one side with round, bare breasts. I shook my head and laughed out loud. Logan turned at the sound, but I didn't acknowledge him. I was busy attaching my new dagger.

Fia had meant to embarrass me, but I was well past that these days. I would wear the damned thing with pride.

WELL, I WOULD HAVE WORN THE DAMNED THING WITH pride, except that Logan insisted I not be openly armed with a weapon I 'didn't know my arse from a hole in the ground about how to use." So I unlooped the leather sheathe from the belt and slipped the entire thing into the deep pocket of my skirts.

It was better than nothing, I supposed.

Besides, the ride to Hagail was tense enough. I was in the center of our group of seven, Sai and Logan on either side of me. Fia rode behind us with Cray, though she kept finding excuses to trot up alongside Logan and stroke his arm. A flash of gray and white caught my eye, almost appearing as if the snow itself were moving. I searched the landscape for whatever it had been, but it had disappeared. Shaking it off, I returned to my discussion with Sai.

The kind man kept up a steady stream of conversation. I wasn't in much of a talking mood, but he didn't require much response from me, and it was better than being left alone with my thoughts.

"Oi, lass! Ye ready tae tell us why ye're goin' tae that godforsaken towne?" Cray interrupted our conversation after a time with a concerned look on his face.

"The rebels took someone we care about." Another flash of gray and white caught my eye.

"Ach. Nasty fellers, those. Well, some of 'em anyway. MacKinnon's lot isn't half bad, they jus' dinna trust the crown."

"So, you're acquainted with the rebels?" Logan cut in.

"We be acquaint'd wi' everythin' in these woods." Cray smiled, pleased he was so knowledgeable.

"Did you see a group of children being brought through here?" I couldn't contain the question. If they knew where the children were, maybe we would be able to save them, too.

The thieves looked at each other. It was Fia who answered.

"A few days ago." There was an uncharacteristic sadness on her features as she spoke the words.

"Do you know where they took them?" I didn't dare to let myself hope.

"No, lass. No one knows where their base be, no' even we." Aengus spoke back to us this time, his head bent low.

Anger surged in my chest. "You say this MacKinnon is a good man? I would hardly say that burning a village and its people to ash, or abducting its children was 'good.'"

"Aye, lass." The air shifted to one of anxious guilt. Most of the men stared ahead, not responding to my words. Eventually, Aengus slowed his horse to fall in line beside me, displacing Sai. "We heard tale o' Bala only yesterday. We dinna ken that the bairns were— tha' they were captives."

"Word is MacKinnon were a better man, but he made the mistake o' workin' wi' Rheisart these past weeks. That man cares for no one and nothing but his own." Cray spoke up to explain their reasonings for not believing the worst of the man.

"Isn't that what you all say?" I couldn't hide the bitterness in my tone.

"Naw. We steal because we have people to take care of, and the crown hasn't bothered to," Sai finally chimed in. The statement caused a murmur of approval from the other men. Fia looked at me curiously, before adding her delayed and more subdued 'Aye.'

It took effort not to bristle at their allegation, but could I argue after everything I had witnessed? I could feel Logan's eyes boring into me, but I didn't turn.

Before I could respond, my six companions tensed, looking off into the woods. I followed their gazes, wondering if the same gray and white flashes I'd been seeing had finally caught their attention. I nervously placed my hand on the dagger Fia had given me, it's unfamiliar weight comforting.

White lightning bolted from the trees and up onto Fia's horse. I jumped, whipping out my knife, embarrassed by the sight of a small marble fox perching on her lap. I quickly returned the blade to my pocket, hoping no one had noticed.

All of the men seemed perfectly accepting of the small animal in their midst. It sat pawing and whimpering at Fia as she studied it for a long moment. She looked from it to the forest, then gave a pointed glance at Aengus.

"Let's move along. T'would seem the trees hav' eyes." Aengus looked around to his men and nodded toward the copse on our right.

The men stared into the same spot and gave their murmur of understanding.

"Someone is watching us?" I asked hesitantly, not able to see any signs of the movement he'd noticed.

"Aye. 'Tis nothin' most like, lass. Probly jus' scouts from another family o' thieves." Cray gave me a smile.

Unease came over me as I contemplated what could be out there. Was it the thieves from yesterday? A predator? After everything we'd already witnessed, I wasn't sure I wanted to find out. I looked ahead as everyone began to nudge their horses into a faster gait.

My eye caught briefly on the small fox nestled behind Fia, perfectly content to be along for the ride before the duo moved to the front of the line. The rest of us quickened our pace, as well, passing the last few hours of the ride in a cautious silence. Even Sai didn't seem to be in much of a talking mood anymore.

I was left with nothing but my own thoughts for company as we continued our journey. By the time we spotted the few tiered buildings of Hagail, my legs and back were stiff, and anxiety pooled in my gut. I stared down at the dilapidated homes, shops, taverns, and inns, unable to control my morbid curiosity about the infamous towne.

None of the warnings could have possibly prepared me for the reality of Hagail.

CHAPTER 35

I barely registered the thieves beginning their farewells as I was so caught up in my first glimpse of Hagail.

"This be where we leave ye, then." Aengus took stock of the towne looming before us. "If ye can, dinna stay too long. 'Tis not a place for the kindly souls ye possess."

He didn't need to convince me. My concern for Oli was the only thing that could propel me forward. The dreadful aura emanating from the neglected towne left me with the urge to disappear back into the safety of the forest.

"Until next time, gorgeous girl." Sai leaned over and planted a shy kiss on my cheek, startling me from my thoughts.

I reached up and placed my hand upon the spot his lips had been, a small blush rising beneath it. His attentions seemed obvious now. I had been so used to belonging to

Oli that I never considered the prospect of someone else finding me desirable.

"Thank you, Sai."

The large, innocent grin I received in response endeared him to me even more.

"You call that a goodbye kiss, boy?" Fia's lilting voice rang out, taking away from the gentle moment.

"This is a proper goodbye." She winked at Sai and me, and then, with a quick, limber movement, she leapt from her horse to Logan's to straddle him. Before anyone could address it, her arms were around his neck and her mouth was over his.

Some of the men laughed, but a few others made gagging noises, including Sai.

I had to look away from the crude scene, not able to stomach Fia's vulgar behavior. That caused her to laugh riotously. She leaned in and whispered something in Logan's ear before dismounting him and landing back on her own horse once more. I didn't think I would ever be able to understand the girl or her motives.

"Thank ye, lass. Truly." Neacal's voice was a welcome relief from the thoughts abounding in my head. His smile was filled with gratitude as he looked at me. "Me family 'ill never forget what ye've done fer our boy."

I gave him a small bow of my head. There would be some in this group that I would miss keenly, and some I would not. Fia blew me a kiss as she turned her horse back toward the forest.

My irritable breaths created short bursts of white fog,

dissipating much more quickly than my mood seemed to be.

Curiously, the small white and gray ball of fur never stirred through it all. I had never seen such a thing. It made the girl all the more puzzling to me that her closest friend appeared to be a fox.

"The Criminals of the Crooked Copse will—" Sai's final farewell ended in a grunt as Cray threw something at the back of his head.

I snorted at the ensuing argument between the two, their voices fading as they got farther away.

After the thieves disappeared back into the trees, I turned to make my way down to Hagail, pulled by some invisible string toward my people. They were suffering. That much was obvious even from a distance. My horse's hooves crunched through filthy snow as I took in the dilapidated storefronts and haunted expressions around me.

"Why didn't you wait for me?" Logan had caught up to me, looking surly as ever.

I ignored his grumbling. If I looked at him for too long, I might punch him. I had been frustrated as it was, but the sight of so many of those who were supposed to be under my protection in this deplorable state was bringing me right up to the edge of reason.

Emaciated children with hollow eyes huddled together. Nude women, no better fed, lounged in storefronts like they were more object than person. They had to be freezing, but it was as though the air had ceased to touch them. One of them stared me down, as if daring me to pass judgment. That was the furthest thing from my mind, though.

Logan took in the same sights with a grim expression, but no surprise. Had he seen things like this before in his capacity as captain? It didn't feel like the time to ask, even if I had felt like speaking to him.

He gestured to the most reputable-looking inn, which was rather like choosing the warmest part of an ice block, and we trotted in that direction. I threw out a few coins to the children before he grabbed my hand.

"Are you trying to get yourself killed? You'll draw unwanted attention doing that."

His high-handed tone was almost as infuriating as the way he had just stopped me from feeding more of these children.

"You are in no position to order me around, Captain."

His face darkened. I felt a petty satisfaction at having brought forth in him some fraction of the rage flowing through my own veins. We didn't speak again as we stabled the horses. We had just gotten the laird's mount back, but I had serious doubts as to whether it would be here come morning. George should fare better, I hoped.

A fight had already broken out in the main room of the inn, and it wasn't yet evening. Lovely. These people were angry, bitter and hardened, and I couldn't blame them. Their anger fueled my own at myself, at Logan, at my father, and at the rebels who burned down villages rather than come to us for solutions.

The innkeeper quoted us a price five times what it should have been. Logan countered, face like a thundercloud. The old man hacked out what might have been a laugh from someone else, then nodded.

"All right, lad. Top floor, second room on the left."

Even the exertion of stomping up the stairs behind Logan did nothing to abate the mounting rage my chronic helplessness had brought forth in me. I couldn't help these people. I hadn't helped find Oli. If anything, I could see now that I had been more of a hindrance. The only thing I had ever been able to do was help my people stay at peace by marrying Oliver. But he had been taken and I hadn't even been able to do that. My breath came in short, furious puffs, and not from the stairs.

I slammed the door. Logan turned, his face reflecting my feelings clearly.

"Please, bring every miscreant in this place down on us."

I narrowed my eyes. "Perhaps I shall. Perhaps I could use a good fight." I knew how unreasonable I sounded, but I couldn't bring myself to care. I felt like a pot about to boil over with the intensity of the emotions swirling in my chest. "The men downstairs seemed to be enjoying themselves."

Logan had the nerve to look skyward with a patronizing sigh. "Well, I don't at all feel like fighting right now, so try to restrain yourself, because I'm afraid your title won't be enough to win you a brawl, Highness." He risked sitting down on the questionable looking bed.

"Indeed, Captain." I said the title like a curse. "It's fortunate your lover gifted me with this dagger, isn't it?" I pulled the weapon out of my pocket, not entirely bluffing about wanting to stab someone.

"My— Is that a naked woman?" He cocked his head to the side.

"Fia seemed to think it fitting." A smirk tugged at my lips, but my eyes still burned.

Logan's eyes moved from the dagger to me, and for a fraction of a second, I thought I saw something more than anger in them. I met his gaze evenly, a challenge in my own. I wasn't sure what I wanted, exactly, except for honesty, answers. Perhaps I only wanted him to be as frustrated as I was.

"Why do you even care about my safety, Logan?" The words were out of my mouth before I could stop them. "We both know you hate me, have hated me for years for reasons you've never bothered to share. Just say it, already."

Logan got to his feet, laughing bitterly.

"You need to hear it that badly? Yes, I do hate you sometimes." He ran a hand irritably over his head.

I took a step back, my eyes burning with more than anger now. I had known that, but hearing it aloud stung more than I wanted to acknowledge.

"Then is this just about ensuring the treaty?" I prodded. "Protecting your brother's property?" The word came out of my mouth unbidden.

I have never felt that way, have I?

I loved Oliver. I had wanted to marry him for as long as I could remember… but that didn't change the wording of the treaty. I was to be "given" to Oliver.

Logan's head snapped up, his eyes blazing with white-hot fury.

"I never said you were anyone's property."

"Yes, well, you didn't have to, did you? The treaty said it for us both. You were content to find fulfillment in your own position while making it perfectly clear how you felt about mine," I spat. "What was it you said? 'Some of us have responsibilities?' Did you think I wasn't aware you were out staving off a war while the only thing expected of me was to look pretty on my wedding day?" I wasn't sure where any of this was coming from. It was like I had released a floodgate from the moment I opened my mouth, but as soon as the words left my lips, I knew they were true. Logan had made his condescension amply apparent.

"You mean, that's all you expected of yourself." He shook his head, jaw clenched. "You *let* them turn you into the simpering princess."

Whatever modicum of self-control I had been holding onto dissolved into the dank tavern air with that comment. The only thing that saved me from exploding was a well-timed knock on the door.

CHAPTER 36

It was the dinner Logan had ordered sent up. It was hard bread and stew with suspicious-looking meat that I was still too cross to question. I forced down a few bites, seething with each swallow. I turned to Logan, who looked as impassive and unperturbed as ever, not even flinching while he wolfed down his own stew.

His complacence fueled my ire more than his comments had. I glared at him.

"I'm surprised you can even see the rest of us from that high horse of yours, Logan." My voice emerged closer to a yell than I had been expecting. "Tell me, how does that holier-than-thou persona factor into you up all night doing god-knows-what with Fia?"

"What?" His soup spoon clattered into his bowl. "What does that have to do with anything?"

"I just find it ironic that the kind of person who would put a woman in that position without thought has the nerve to judge anyone." I got to my feet, pacing. Men could have their fun and leave, but women had to bear the consequences. Logan, having been raised by a single village woman, should know that better than anyone.

That brought his fury back in full force. He put his bowl aside and stood up, practically growling now.

"First of all, I am confident that Fia was no' in a position she didn't wish to be in." He stepped closer to me. "And don't you think that's a bit hypocritical. What about your precious Oli?"

Now it was my turn to be confused. *Is he suggesting what I think he is?*

"Not that it's any of your business, but if you're insinuating what I believe you are, then no. There is no hypocrisy there. Oliver and I never..." My cheeks flamed, and I couldn't meet Logan's eyes. *Why am I explaining myself to him?*

Logan let out a short snort of disbelief.

"Well, if that's true, that would make yours the only skirt he didn't charm his way into." He pressed his lips together and closed his eyes, like he hadn't meant to say that. Because it wasn't true? Or because it was?

Oliver and I had been promised to one another since before we were born. Who would even consent to be with him, knowing that?

I shook my head in denial, backing away. If he had wanted me to stop talking, he had succeeded in stealing my words.

"Did you say that just to hurt me?" I finally asked.

His eyes tightened with remorse, and his shoulders

slumped. "I said it because I was angry. I'm sorry, Charlie." He looked sincere, but I didn't care.

I turned away, staring at the wall rather than his face.

"Charlie," I breathed. "Fine time to actually call me by my name." I glared up at him, clinging to my anger, so I wouldn't have to think about what he had just said. My own renewed ire seemed to ignite his.

"Why is that so important to you?" He put his hands up, covering the distance I had put between us. "It's not even your real name."

For some reason, that pushed me over whatever precipice I was standing on. "It's the only name I give a damn about!" I snapped.

Logan stilled, his features morphing into an unreadable mask. He opened his mouth, but whatever he was about to say was cut off by another pounding on the door.

CHAPTER 37

"There be a problem with your horse, mi'laird." The innkeeper's phlegmy voice came through the thin door.

Has someone already stolen the destrier? I hadn't expected it to last until morning, but that was fast.

Logan motioned for me to stand back, then opened the door.

"The mare be hurt. Someone tried tae make off wi' her, did a poor job of it."

Logan glanced back at me, the indecision clear in his eyes. Would I be safer at his side or in a locked room? I watched him weigh his options.

"Stay here." His mouth was grim. "Lock the door. I won't be long."

"Then I'll just come with you." My heart was still pounding from our argument, but I didn't want to be separated if there was danger.

He clenched his jaw in frustration.

"Damn it, woman. Can you just do as I ask, this once?"

I scowled at him, ready to refuse. He sighed.

"Please, Charlie," he said in a softer tone.

I looked away.

"Very well," I said after a time. "I'll stay."

Logan nodded, then turned to follow the innkeeper. I locked the door behind him, true to my word. For several minutes, I paced the tiny space, focusing on the sound of my footsteps rather than every anxious, panicked thought assaulting my mind.

I let out a relieved whoosh of air when I heard the key turning in the lock. Of course, Logan's presence would bring with it a different sort of anxiety after our earlier confrontation, but better that than this. The door swung open, and I turned to face him, shoulders squared.

But it wasn't Logan.

An enormous black-haired man filled the doorway, another fairer-haired one barely visible behind him. The blood drained from my face. I scarcely had time to scream before the hulking man was in front of me, one greasy palm over my mouth and the other wrapping me tightly to him.

The fairer-haired one closed the door quietly behind him, before stalking around to the other side of me. Something about him seemed familiar. My skin crawled with the idea that I knew him somehow.

The man holding me spun me around to face his friend, whispering threats in my ear. His hot breath made each word feel as if they were sticking to my skin. "If you so much as whimper, we'll gut you, and claim it was your boyfriend that did it." Slowly, he slid his hand from my mouth, downwards, groping my chest as he moved to secure both of my arms in his hands.

"I would leave now if I were you. My friend will be back any moment, and he will kill you for this." Of that, I had no doubt.

"Don't worry. He'll be comin' along." The men laughed at the unspoken jest between them.

Is Logan being attacked as well? Cold tendrils of fear gripped my insides.

The fair one removed a dagger from his belt, flipping it in his hand to prove the other's point. Each flick of his wrist showcased the natural skill he possessed. Something in the movement made my mind reel. I knew him. This was Graham, the Luanian kingsman who escaped. The rebel. Panic rushed through my veins.

My face must have given me away.

"Look, Douglas. The Princess seems to remember me."

He walked by me and touched his dagger to the tip of my chin. "You know who I am, Princess? Surprised you would recognize a lowly guard like me." With a wink, he flicked the tip of my nose before walking away.

Maybe I wouldn't have recognized him had I not been riding alongside him days ago. But he didn't know that.

His friend tightened his grip, and my arms stung from the pressure. I knew that I would have bruises just above my elbows, but that was the least of my problems. At least I had my hands free. I put my right hand in my pocket. The men didn't notice or care, likely not perceiving me as any kind of threat.

I gripped the curvy hilt, familiar now from the ride I spent with my hand on it.

At least Fia is good for something.

I clutched the handle tightly, waiting for a moment I might be able to use it. Douglas was shrugging at something that Graham said, relaxing his hold slightly. This might be the only chance I would get. I kept the dagger in my pocket and slowly worked it out of its scabbard. Just having my hand around it made me bolder. I ground my hips back against my captor, receiving the desired effect of loosening his arms even more.

"Ooh, I like that. Maybe having you at camp will be more fun than I thought." The man's breath was hot against my neck once more.

Positioning the dagger just so, I thrust my hips backward, putting considerably more force into it this time. I prayed the blade would be sharp enough to cut through my skirts as well as his skin.

The man cried out in pain and shoved me to the floor. I looked up to see him clutching his manhood, blood soaking the fabric of his trousers. I

pulled the dagger from my pocket, ready to use it again if necessary, then scrambled toward the door on my hands and knees.

Acute pain jarred my body as I was forcibly kicked in the stomach. I tumbled over, hitting my head on the small table next to the bed. I tried to crawl away, but my body seized.

Graham watched impassively as his injured friend kicked again and again. Each blow made my vision blacken a little at the edges. There was a split second of relief, and I thought maybe he was finished. Then, Douglas picked me up by my hair with one hand and used his bloody fist to punch my face with the other.

As he doubled over from the strain of lifting me, I fell to the ground.

The traitor stepped up to intervene. Graham roughly placed a gag in my mouth and bound my hands behind my back. He threw me over his shoulder, and we left the room.

As much pain as I was in, there was a small satisfaction in watching the limping giant clutch what was left of his manhood.

At least I hadn't gone down without a fight.

THE ARAMACH

My vision was blurred as I opened my eyes. The gentle light of dawn was beginning to creep through the snowy canopy. People moved about, speaking in quick, angry tones. Each syllable uttered caused my temples to throb. The pounding thrum echoed in time with the painful spasms wracking my body.

I stared at the large tree next to me, trying to draw comfort from its steady and ancient presence. But there was none to be found. This part of the forest felt more like a cage than a sanctuary. I turned my head away, pain forging its way through the muscles in my stiff neck and back.

My eyes burned, and my vision was spotty as I tried to focus on the camp. I closed them once more and took deep steadying breaths, concentrating on the feeling of snow gently landing on my face. A coughing fit overtook me. My lungs weren't quite ready for that much air just yet.

The delicate white flakes continued to fall, cooling the swollen and split skin every place they settled. The small solace it brought me was at odds with the reality that I found myself in.

I shivered. It was freezing, but I couldn't force myself to move from where the men had dumped me.

My hands were raw, burning beneath the rope binding them.

I had been laying on them for too long, but there was little chance I'd be able to roll over any time soon.

My stomach was still roiling from the pain it had endured at the inn. I was sure Douglas had broken at least one of my ribs.

The ride here hadn't offered any reprieve.

I've never ridden on a horse in this manner. I had thought with dark humor.

The men had tied me over the back of their mount. The assault to my abdomen had continued with each galloping step, making me weak with agony. As soon as they dumped me to the ground, I lost the contents of my stomach.

I wheezed on a dry laugh as I remembered what Douglas had looked like when he told the men what had happened to him. I could see clearly the way his pants were covered in blood and how pale his skin had been.

At least I hadn't been the only one in pain on that ride.

I coughed again, my body crumpling with pain in response. The cycle continued. Each cough caused excruciating pain; the pain, in turn, made me cough. The torturous cycle continued until my vision blackened almost entirely.

I wondered briefly if I would die there. *Will I die before knowing if Logan survived? Before knowing if Oliver is still out there? Will I die before...*

"Charlie?"

The voice stopped me mid-thought. I would recognize it anywhere.

"Charlie?!"

I painfully turned my head to look in the direction of the panicked whispering.

I could barely make out his features, but I knew those midwinter-blue eyes.

"Oli?"

A MESSAGE FROM US

We need your help!

Did you know that authors, in particular indie authors like us, make their living on reviews?

If you liked this book, or even if you didn't, please take a moment to let people know on Amazon, Goodreads, and/or Bookbub!

Remember, reviews don't have to be long.

It can be as simple as your preferred star rating and an: 'I loved it!' or: 'Not my cup of tea…'

So please, take a moment to let us know what you think. We depend on *your* feedback!

Now that that's out of the way, if you want to come shenanigate with us, rant and rave about these books and others, get access to awesome giveaways, exclusive content and some pretty ridiculous live videos, come join us on Facebook here: https://www.facebook.-com/groups/driftersandwanderers

For even more freebies and some behind-the-scenes content, you can also sign up for Robin's newsletter here: https://www.subscribepage.com/robindmahlenewsletter_tse

ELBIN ACKNOWLEDGMENTS

Robin Acknowledgments:

A huge thank you to my sister, Veronica, for coming to save my sanity during the making of this book. Elle, writing this book with you has been an adventure. I love the world and the characters we've crafted together, and I can't wait to write the rest of the series together. To my husband, the other half of my writing team, thank you for plotting with us and watching our monsters so I could churn out these pages. Thank you to Brianna for managing half of my life and helping Winter's Captive come into being, and Jamie for once again saving our procrastinating butts with your last- minute proofreading. There are too many amazing, supportive people in my life to mention them all by name, but I am so incredibly grateful for the help every step of the way. Our beta and ARC readers and early fans, there would be no point in writing at all without all of you. Thank you for starting this writing journey with me!

Elle Acknowledgments:

Thank you to everyone who made this possible. I know I will forget to mention some of you by name, but I am so appreciative of everything you've done! Brianna, Jamie, and all of our supportive author friends in groups like AAYA and YABS -- Thank you! You have made this first-time author's journey so much easier. Robin, this has been an amazing adventure so far, and I am so grateful you brought me along. I love how much our friendship has shone through Charlie and Isla. You're my octopus. Thank you to my amazing husband! I couldn't have done this without your support. Your creative input and taking care of our boys, along with the occasional box of wine to calm my nerves, were invaluable. I love you more than all the words in all the books in all the world. Thank you, Jill, for going on this crazy adventure with us and being so supportive. I am so grateful I have you in my life. To the woman who taught me to read... your patience and love throughout my life has meant the world to me. I love you so much. Thank you for always being my biggest supporter in everything I do. And finally, to each person who has picked this book up and loved it as much as we do, thank you. Your enthusiasm and support keep us going. You guys are the best.

ABOUT THE AUTHORS

Elle and Robin can usually be found on road trips around the US haunting taco-festivals and taking selfies with unsuspecting Spice Girls impersonators.

They have a combined PH.D in Faery Folklore and keep a romance advice column under a British pen-name for raccoons. They have a rare blood type made up solely of red wine and can only write books while under the influence of the full moon.

Between the two of them they've created a small army of insatiable humans and when not wrangling them into their cages, they can be seen dancing jigs and sacrificing brownie batter to the pits of their stomachs.

And somewhere between their busy schedules, they still find time to create words and put them into books.

ALSO BY ELLE & ROBIN

The Lochlann Treaty Series:

Winter's Captive

Spring's Rising

Summer's Rebellion

Autumn's Reign

The Lochlann Feuds Series:

Scarlet Princess

Tarnished Crown

Crimson Kingdom

Obsidian Throne

Twisted Pages Series:

Of Thorns and Beauty

Of Beasts and Vengeance

Of Glass and Ashes

Of Thieves and Shadows

The World Apart Series By Robin D. Mahle:

The Fractured Empire

The Tempest Sea

The Forgotten World

The Ever Falls

Unfabled Series:

Promises and Pixie Dust

Made in the USA
Coppell, TX
16 December 2023

26253288R10152